THE HORN OF MORTAL DANGER

Lawrence Leonard is a distinguished musician. He began playing the cello at the age of five, won a scholarship to the Royal Academy at fifteen and was a Proms' performer a year later. He later went on to study conducting in Paris. His many musical achievements include responsibility for the London premiere of *West Side Story*, the composition of a tone poem for the occasion of the Sultan of Oman's birthday, and the creation of a music-theatre piece called *What the Waiter Saw*, which was staged in 1987.

The Horn of Mortal Danger, a classic fantasy, is Lawrence Leonard's only children's book and was a completely new departure for him. He wrote it because "there is nothing more enjoyable than an exciting story. I didn't think it was for children particularly; everyone thrills to adventure."

Born in London, Lawrence Leonard has travelled widely throughout his life, but has come to rest for the moment in Box Hill, Surrey.

The Horn of Mortal Danger

Lawrence Leonard

WALKER BOOKS
LONDON

To Jenifer and Simon

Technical assistance from
Mr George Bridges
is gratefully acknowledged

First published 1980 by Julia MacRae Books
A division of Walker Books Ltd, 87 Vauxhall Walk, London SE11 5HJ

© 1980 Lawrence Leonard
Cover and map illustrations by Gavin Rowe

This edition published 1989

Printed in Great Britain by Cox and Wyman Ltd, Reading

British Library Cataloguing in Publication Data
Leonard, Lawrence
The horn of mortal danger.
I. Title
823'.914[F]
ISBN 0-7445-0847-9

Contents

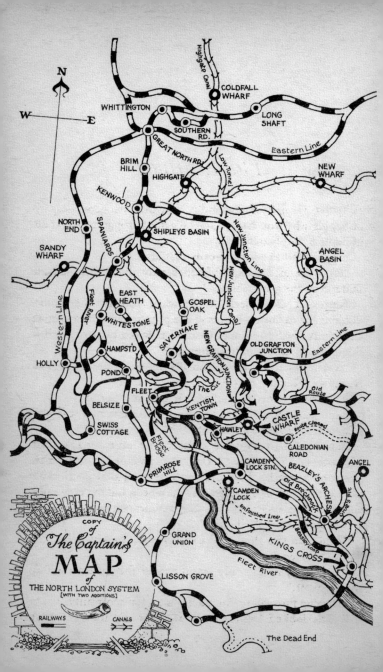

1

The Railway

"What I *can't* understand," said Mrs Widgeon despairingly, "is why you had to start digging through to Australia in Dad's potato patch."

"Well, I had to start somewhere, didn't I?"

"What Mum means, Widgie, is why didn't you choose that bit by the garden shed?"

"Oh shut up, Jen; I hate it when you use that voice. Because the earth was softer in the potato patch if you must know. Anyway how was I to tell it was a potato patch if there weren't any potatoes showing?"

"You can't really have thought you could dig through to Australia, Widgie."

"Someone will one day," said Widgie stubbornly.

Mrs. Widgeon took the plug out of the kitchen sink and dried her hands on a tea-towel.

"Look, Widgie, I don't want to be unreasonable, but what am I going to say to Dad when he comes home? You know he spent a whole Sunday preparing that patch with peat and all sorts of things, and he's been talking ever since about how wonderful it'll be to have our own potatoes—"

"Alright, Mum, I'm *sorry*."

"And then you throw the earth all over the bluebells."

"They're weeds."

"Well, they're the only bit of colour the garden's got at the moment."

"Digging through to Australia," said Jen scornfully.

Widgie looked from one to the other and for a moment

the corners of his mouth tugged down; then he opened the kitchen door, slammed it behind him and stumped out of the house.

"I suppose it is a bit hard when we both get at him," said Mrs. Widgeon.

"But think of Dad when he sees the wreckage."

"I do," she said, sharply. "Oh well—you'd better go upstairs and mend your sweater or something, Jen; it's all holes and so are your jeans."

Jen sighed dramatically and went upstairs to her bedroom, which was next door to the one Widgie shared with his hamsters. She wrinkled her nose at them as she passed, and remembered too late that she'd promised herself not to do that because of the danger of distorting it. She looked at it in the mirror. Her nose didn't seem to be getting any worse; it just wasn't satisfactory, particularly next to Widgie's, which was definitely and indisputably superior.

She gave a shrug of resignation and dragged her sweater out of the drawer.

Widgie was still standing outside the house, staring at the garden gate and kicking it while he rehearsed a new and improved version of the great potato patch controversy. Perhaps, if he apologised properly and made good the damage, he could persuade them to call him by his real name—Simon Widgeon—instead of that beastly 'Widgie'. He doubted it though. He thrust his hands deep into his trouser pockets in frustrated rage and something hard and metallic forced its way through a small hole, slithered down his leg and rolled onto the pavement. It was a 10p piece left over from Friday's school-lunch money, and Widgie couldn't help grinning at the fine irony of it all. He picked it up and began walking down to the shops at the end of the road, already partly reconciled to the injustices that had been heaped upon him.

He realized that what he really needed more than anything else at the moment was a bar of chocolate, so he went into the stationer's and bought one, and as he unwrapped it he thought that perhaps he would go for a walk up the hill to the pet shop next to the cinema and see if they had any new hamsters in.

It was a nice afternoon. The sun was shining, and Widgie began to feel like poking around in an inquisitive sort of manner on his way up. Usually he didn't do this because he had got into the habit of being in a hurry, but this time he took his time, and that was how he came to notice the little gate on the left near the top of the hill.

"Funny—I never saw that before," he said to himself, and he pushed it open. It led to some very tumbledown old steps that curved round out of sight, and he thought that perhaps he would wander down them and see where they went.

They meandered down a grassy embankment for a little while and ended up at what had once been a Railway Station. It hadn't been one for a long while, though, for the platform was in a terrible mess and the brown wooden benches were broken and peeling and the Waiting Room windows were cracked.

Widgie found it quite interesting, in fact almost exciting, he decided. He stared around at it all for a few minutes and then he got down onto where the railway lines had once been. They left a wide and often green path that appeared to cut right across the streets he knew so well—it was like a secret world that no-one had any further use for, and the more Widgie looked at it the more possibilities it seemed to have.

So he turned back and ran up the steps two at a time and then down the hill to the shops and back to the house.

"Jen," he shouted as soon as he got in.

"Feet!" called Mrs. Widgeon automatically, from the kitchen.

Widgie went back and wiped his feet on the mat and Jen came downstairs still trying to mend her sweater.

"Jen, come out—I've found something."

There was a most un-Widgielike sound to Widgie's voice, so she stared at him for a moment and then put her half-mended sweater on the hall-stand.

"I'm just going out with Widgie for a moment, Mum."

Mrs Widgeon looked as though she was going to object, but she was concentrating on making the pastry for a tart and wondering what to put in it, and she decided not to.

"Well, put your coat on then—you've still got a bit of that cold left, don't forget."

So Widgie put on his as well to keep her company, and then he bundled her out of the house, up the hill, through the gate and down the steps onto the messy platform.

"There."

"Wow!" said Jen and Widgie felt quite proud, as if it belonged to him.

"Come and look at the Booking Office," he said, so they went over to it and pushed the side door open. They had to tiptoe in very carefully because the floor was rotted away in places.

"There's even some old tickets," said Jen, pulling one out of its little rack and looking at it. "Cranley Gardens to Alexandra Palace—Twopence," she read. "Fancy that."

They opened all the drawers and cupboards and there were all sorts of interesting things in them like old woollen gloves, and chipped cups with the dregs of tea made long ago, and yellow official forms that were no use any more. Rather sad, thought Jen.

Then they went out again and Widgie let her stare around for a bit before they climbed down onto the tracks.

"Which way?" asked Jen, peering to the right where they went under the bridge with the road on top, and then to the left where they curved out of sight.

"Let's go round the curve," said Widgie, as she had known he would, and so together they took their first steps along the old and disused railway.

"It won't be half as exciting with a torch. Come on; we needn't go far."

Widgie found Jen's arm and pulled her in after him. Jen really felt worried, but she knew Widgie in this mood and the last thing she wanted at this point was a row, so she allowed herself to be pulled, and together they entered the blacker tunnel.

As well as being very black it seemed to be going downhill, and this interested them greatly—was it going to the bowels of the earth perhaps?

"I bet we get to Australia," said Widgie.

"More likely we're underneath Muswell Hill Broadway."

"I can see a bit now." Widgie peered hard at Jen. "I can see your nose anyway."

"I bet you can," said Jen bitterly. "Trust you to mention that. Well, I'll tell you what, I'm not going any further. I don't like it here one bit, and if you're going to be rotten on top of it—"

Widgie sighed to himself.

"I can see your hair as well," he said, hoping to make things better. "Anyway, let's just go another... hey, there's something on the ground here."

He bent down and groped around. "Here it is—it's a hat."

He held it up for inspection and they both felt it all over.

"So it is," said Jen. "Isn't it small!"

"It's a funny shape as well. It's like those hats coalmen wear to stop the coal falling down their necks."

"It smells of coal, too. How odd." Jen sniffed it and peered around. Suddenly she grabbed Widgie's arm. "What's that down there?"

"Where?"

"Lower down—half way up the wall on the right. There's a glow—can you see it?"

They shuffled farther down the tunnel and there *was* a glow, getting brighter as they got nearer, and underneath it there was a long thing propped against the wall. When they got up to it, Jen felt the wall gingerly. "I've got it, Widgie. It's a lamp standing on a shelf—wait a minute while I see if there's a handle. There."

She held it aloft.

"There's not much light," said Widgie critically. "Can you turn it up?"

"I don't think it does—it's an oil lamp but it doesn't have anything to adjust the wick. Still, it's better than nothing—we can at least see something now."

"The thing underneath is a shovel," said Widgie. He picked it up. "That's funny—the handle's still warm as if someone had just been using it. Creepy." He felt little prickles going up and down his spine. Suddenly he gave a shout: "Is anyone there?"

But no-one answered.

"For goodness sake," said Jen, startled. "You gave me a fright."

"Come on, Jen, let's go farther in now we've got the lamp. Hold it higher."

The lamp threw long flickering shadows on the wall, but it did little to light the floor, and suddenly Widgie, who was in front, flung out a protective arm and pushed Jen back.

"What *are* you doing?" she said irritably. "I nearly dropped the lamp."

"Come and look. It's a pit or something—I nearly fell in."

Jen edged forwards until she was next to Widgie.

"I say, be careful. That's awfully dangerous."

"It's got a ladder," said Widgie feeling round it with great excitement. "It's made of iron, I think. Look, I've got my hand on the top of it."

"Well I don't care what it's made of—I'm not going down. Come on Widgie, we've done enough for one day. We'll come back tomorrow with a torch."

"Oh please, Jen. It may not even be here tomorrow."

Widgie had suddenly got determination, and nothing

could hold him now. He grasped the top rung and swung himself down into the blackness, going who knows where, and began feeling with his feet.

"Widgie," said Jen in a commanding voice—after all, she was older—and then she thought, well, I can't leave him down there with no light, so she followed him, holding the lantern with one hand and hanging on with the other.

"Hey, mind my fingers," said Widgie, crossly.

Jen trod more carefully.

"Maybe it's a well—there may be water at the bottom."

"I don't think so—the wall isn't even damp."

"It *looks* like a well. Are you counting the rungs?"

"Yes, I'm at twenty-three."

"Well, I'm not going down forever."

Silence from a determined Widgie, and then a shout.

"I've got there, Jen. It's only earth."

Jen almost fell the last few rungs in anxiety and when she reached the bottom, Widgie was already exploring. She held the lantern up.

"Careful, there may be another."

"Another what?"

"Another pit."

Widgie hadn't thought of that, so he stopped for a moment.

"Can you get the light in a better place? It's not shining on the floor enough." She put it down. "Yes, that's better. Hey, look at that—there's a bump in the floor over this side. Quite a big one."

Jen came over and had a look.

"Why it's only earth," she said, feeling somehow cheated.

"Yes, but it's solid. You feel it."

Jen patted it all over—it was about two feet high and rounded, and. . .

"It's got a hole in the middle," she said.

"Has it?" said Widgie interested. "Put your hand in it."

"It's quite small and there's a—yes, there's a hook in the middle. Shall I pull it?"

"Wait a sec," said Widgie, too late, for she had already pulled it.

There was a very loud, grating noise and they felt the whole pit vibrating. Nothing seemed to be happening, but the noise went on and on as if someone was grinding up a lot of metal. They both looked wildly at one another and then Widgie saw the thing moving in the dim lamp-light.

"The ladder," he shouted, and they both rushed over and grabbed it.

"Push," gasped Widgie, and they pushed and pushed upwards as hard as they could, but it was no use. Quite slowly, but with great determination, the ladder lowered itself into the floor beneath them until only one rung was exposed. Then the noise stopped.

"Oh *Jen*."

They both stared at the one rung and Jen almost felt like crying—as if it wasn't enough to see the ladder go without being blamed for it as well. She went back to the hook and tried to push it down, but it wouldn't move.

"What can we do?" she moaned, and they both sat on the bump and thought.

"*Someone* will come if we shout loud enough," said Widgie suddenly, and he began to shout "help" as loudly as he could.

After a few moments, he said "Why aren't you shouting?"

"I was thinking instead," said Jen, chasing hard after a back-of-the-mind thought. "You see, if that hook lowers the ladder it can't be to stop people like us getting out—there wouldn't be any sense in that. It must be to stop people down here from being followed—in which case there's more to this pit than meets the eye."

She got up and walked over to the slit through which the ladder had disappeared.

"It's just a slit—there's only room for the ladder." She peered round. "Come and help me feel the walls."

They both began feeling the walls all over and as high as

they could, with the help of the lantern, but by the time
they'd got back to where they'd started there had been no
openings nor anything odd about them.

"Let's try the hook again," said Widgie, so they both
went over to it and pushed and pushed, but it wouldn't
budge.

"I know. Maybe it's slotted into a groove or something.
Let's try knocking it sideways."

They wrestled with it in all directions until they were
both sweaty and cross, but they couldn't make it do anything.

"Oh, it's useless," said Jen. "If only we had a hammer."

"That's a good idea."

Widgie thought a moment and then he climbed on top of
the bump and gave it an almighty kick.

"Ow!" shouted Widgie, nursing his foot, and the hook fell
smartly back into place.

How wonderful it was to hear the grating noise start up
again and to watch the ladder slowly climbing up the wall.
Jen grabbed the lantern, and almost before the ladder had
stopped they were rushing up the rungs two at a time, and
when they got to the top they practically flung themselves
into the passage in case it changed its mind and went down
again. But it didn't, and even the sloping tunnel looked
almost friendly now.

They peered back for a moment into the pit.

How odd to take so much trouble over it, thought
Widgie.

"Come on," said Jen. "I'm starving, and you've got to
face the music from Dad about the potatoes."

"Thanks for reminding me."

They decided to leave the lantern where they'd found it,
on the shelf in the wall, and then they went, quite quickly
this time, uphill to the end of the passage. They turned left
at the disused tunnel and finally came out of it into the
open air, where they stood for a moment, blinking in the

evening sunlight.

"Not a word when we get home," said Widgie.

"But what about our clothes? Anyway we shouldn't tell Mum any lies."

"I don't mean *lies*, silly. We'll just say we went down the embankment and played on the old tracks. Then we can come back tomorrow."

For Widgie was determined that they hadn't seen the last of the pit, and nor indeed had they.

2

The Pit

The next morning it was raining. Jen went into Widgie's room and they looked out of his bedroom window in dismay.

"Mum will *never* let us play on the tracks in the rain," said Jen miserably.

They washed and dressed disconsolately and went down to breakfast, where Widgie cheered up a bit because it was cheese on toast—his favourite.

"You'd better use up the morning clearing out your bedrooms," said Mrs. Widgeon. "They're an absolute mess."

They looked at each other hopelessly and began clearing up the breakfast things; then they went upstairs, dragging their feet, and made a start on Widgie's.

"Come on," said Jen trying to be cheerful, "Let's get it all done quickly and then maybe it'll stop raining."

So they set to, putting things in cupboards and under the beds, and by ten o'clock they had finished, even including cleaning out the hamsters' cage.

"What shall we do now?" asked Widgie in a voice filled with irony.

Jen looked out of the window.

"There you are—told you so," she said proudly, and when he looked out he saw that not only had the rain stopped but that the sun was trying to come through in a watery sort of way.

They rushed down to the kitchen, and Widgie managed to get there first.

"Can we go out and play now, Mum? It's stopped raining. Oh—and do you think we could have a thermos of tea and some sandwiches so that we can stay out till tea-time?"

"Did you do your rooms?" she asked, putting on the kettle and getting out some sliced bread.

"Yes, Mum—really we did, even the hamsters; you go and look."

So there was a lot of getting-things-ready, as Jen called it, with Mum making sandwiches and Widgie going off on mysterious little errands of his own, until eventually they got out, with Widgie carrying a plastic shopping bag containing the thermos and some ham sandwiches, under which he had hidden a coal shovel, a hammer, a torch and some string.

"Why string?" asked Jen, interested.

"So that when we go in wherever we go from the pit, we can tie it to the hook and make sure we can find our way back."

Jen thought this very clever of Widgie, and she also liked his unspoken thought that the pit must lead somewhere and not be just a pit.

This time the journey to the iron gate was child's play, but when they got there it was firmly shut, much to their surprise.

"That's funny, I thought we left it open."

Widgie gave it a shove and looked at it blankly.

"It won't open." He felt for the padlock. "It's locked. Someone's locked it."

"What a swiz."

"But who on earth could it be?"

"Oh, I don't know," said Jen crossly. "Some busybody from the railway. We shouldn't have left it open, then he wouldn't have noticed it."

"Well, it seems odd to me considering there *isn't* a railway any more. Anyway, we can't let a little thing like this stop us—we'll just have to tackle the padlock."

Widgie rummaged in his plastic bag and got out the hammer.

"You'll never do it with that," said Jen, "it's a jolly heavy padlock."

"Well, I'm not going home again to fetch whatever you fetch to open padlocks, so it'll just have to do," and he gave it a terrific whack.

"You'll wake the dead," said Jen, as the sound rolled round the tunnel.

Widgie banged it again, and then again even harder, and then he lost his temper with it and he banged it and banged it in all directions until the top of the hammer came off and flew into the little tunnel behind the bars.

"Oh golly," he moaned, "that's torn it."

Jen could hear that he was near tears, so she used her comforting voice.

"Never mind—I'll find something." She kicked around the tunnel for a bit and came back with a largish chunk of rock. "Here—try this."

Widgie went over to the attack again, hurling the rock at the padlock from about three feet away; and then going up to it and banging it very fast from close quarters, but apart from looking a bit of a wreck, the padlock stayed locked.

Then Widgie tried levering the iron loop upwards with the handle of the hammer and eventually it went. *Snap!*

"I've done it," he yelled triumphantly, and he proceeded to disentangle the chain and push open the gate. It creaked rustily.

"Well done," said Jen admiringly.

They switched on the torch and went in, carefully shutting the door behind them this time and trying to arrange the battered padlock so that it looked as if it was doing its job. After they had gone in about twenty paces Jen flashed the torch around, and there was an empty niche.

"Look. The lantern's gone."

"What an extraordinary thing. So has the hat and the

shovel. Someone *has* been here."

They shone the torch everywhere but there was no sign of them.

"It's not a very nice thought, is it?" whispered Jen.

They stood absolutely still and listened. There wasn't a sound anywhere, except for a slight creak every now and then from the gate.

"I hope whoever it is doesn't lock that gate again."

"They'd have to get a new padlock if they did," said Widgie, in his normal voice. "Come on, Jen. I'm jolly well not going to be swindled out of our adventure by a rotten old hat and shovel. And we've got the torch now, so we don't need the lantern."

They walked on to the pit, and when they got there they examined it carefully from the top before going down.

"The tunnel *does* go on the other side of the pit," said Jen, flashing her torch ahead. "See—there's a narrow walkway by the tunnel wall. *And* it still slopes downwards."

But Widgie was busy looking at his pit.

"It's very well made, but everything's a bit smaller than usual—the bricks and the ladder, I mean."

"I'd love to go on down the tunnel and see where it goes."

"Well, maybe later. We can't do everything at once. Shine the torch for me, Jen, while I get on the ladder, and then I'll shine it for you."

They climbed down to the bottom and propped the food bag against the wall, and Jen held the torch while Widgie attacked the bump with his coal shovel. The earth was very thin all round it, and it was bone dry so that it came away in large chunks.

"Look at that," said Jen, shining the torch over the bit Widgie had cleared.

"It's made of iron plates and they're hardly even rusty."

"Really strong they are, too—they're bolted together with iron bolts."

After a bit, Jen had a go, and in about half-an-hour there it stood—nothing more than a largish bump with a hole in the top for a hook.

"Let's have some tea," said Widgie; so they sat on it and unscrewed the thermos, passing the plastic cup from one to the other while Jen shone the torch all round the walls to make sure they hadn't missed anything.

"Have another look at the slit for the ladder, Jen."

"It's just a slit."

"Someone took so much trouble over it all there must be *something* we've missed."

"Well, I hope we don't have to shovel up the floor next."

"It is a bit hopeless." Widgie took the torch and shone it all round the slit, and Jen bent down to look.

"Wait a minute—shine it here."

Widgie brought the torch nearer and Jen got down on hands and knees. Neatly inscribed in the brickwork above the slit, in capital letters, were the words DOWN LINE. BREAK UP.

They felt a rush of excitement. "What *can* they mean," said Widgie, his voice all of a tremble.

Jen stood up and stared at it, saying to herself, "Think, you silly girl, *think*," and then she had a blinding flash of inspiration, so absolutely brilliant and pure in its logic that she tingled all over.

"The ladder," she said in a squeaky voice. "The ladder— don't you remember? There was one rung sticking up and it stuck up right next to that brick."

Widgie stared at her—what a girl, what a brain, what intelligence, what. . .

"That's the one at the top now," he said. "Honestly, I'm not keen on pulling that hook again."

"Don't be a silly," said Jen excitedly. "I'll climb up and look at it. You stay here."

She grabbed the torch and started up the ladder, and when she had got there she began examining the top-most rung.

Widgie felt funny being left alone in the dark pit, so he sat on the bump for comfort and watched her fiddling away.

"There *is* something different about it," came Jen's voice. "It's got a join in the middle. I say, Widgie, it pushes up. It's alright to tread on but it breaks upwards. That's what they meant. I wonder what—yes it's hollow, it's got a hole right through it."

"Look inside it then," Widgie called out, trying not to expect too much.

"I've got—I've got it," squeaked Jen. "It's a key, there's a key inside it. Wait a minute—yes, I've got it."

"Push the rung back."

"I have." Jen clambered down and they both examined her find. It was quite an old key rather like the one they used for the garden shed at home but much smaller.

"All we need now is a key-hole," said Widgie, meaning to be funny.

"Yes, and I bet I know where it'll be. I bet it's in one of those bolts on the bump."

Widgie was so taken aback by Jen's second brain-wave that he couldn't even think of an answer, so he went over to the bump, and together they began examining every bolt in turn.

"*There* you are," said Jen triumphantly, after they'd looked at about thirty of them. "I knew we'd find it."

It was a small key-hole fitted into one of the bolts, and as Jen put the key in they both felt quite odd, as if they had discovered somebody else's secret. So much so that they looked up guiltily to the top of the pit in case someone was watching them. Did they see or imagine the dim outline of a face pulled back suddenly?

"No," said Widgie firmly. "No-one there. Does it turn, Jen?"

"Well, I think it will, with a bit of effort, but I don't much feel like doing it after that ladder business. I mean, you never know *what* might happen."

Widgie stood up and considered.

"I don't feel like it much either, but we'll never be satisfied until we do, I suppose. Look, Jen, you go and stand by the ladder and get ready to jump up it and I'll try to turn it."

"No, we'd better stay together," said Jen bravely, "but you turn it."

Widgie knelt over the bump and began wiggling the key this way and that. It was pretty stiff, but eventually he got the slots right, and stood up so as to be ready to jump back from whatever it was.

He turned it full circle.

There was a metallic creaking noise and very slowly indeed the bump began to open like a hatch being pushed up from inside. It really made very little noise, and when it was standing upright like the top of an opened tin, it gave a small sigh of compressed air and flopped backwards onto the floor behind it, leaving them staring into a large hole.

A dim light shone from inside. They crept forward, peering down together. They were both so utterly mystified by what they saw that they couldn't move for a moment.

They just stared with their mouths open.

"A railway," whispered Widgie.

"A tiny one," said Jen.

They stood back and looked at each other in amazement.

"It can't be," said Widgie, and they crept forward again.

But it was—a very neat, perfect little railway, and really not so little after all. Widgie could see that the top of the engine would be quite a bit taller than him. Everything was exactly right—the station had two platforms either side of the double tracks, with a footbridge going from one to the other and there were even beautifully painted signs saying things like LONG SHAFT STATION; WAITING ROOM; GENTS and BOOKING OFFICE.

The engine had twelve trucks behind it—some were open, some had tarpaulin coverings and some were real vans, including a proper Guard's Van at the end. The rails were about two feet apart and the sleepers were made of thick wood with tiny chips of gravel as a foundation. At one end of the platform was a bunker full of coal, with a big pile of wood next to it.

There were no people.

"Let's climb down," whispered Jen. "Do you think the bump will close again?"

"Not if we don't pull anything," said Widgie, deliberately loudly.

"Sshh," said Jen, frightened.

But no-one came.

"How shall we get down?" said Jen. "It's too far to jump —it's about twenty feet."

"There must be some way." Widgie flashed his torch inside the bump. "I bet that's it."

He bent down to look, and there, hooked onto some large nails round the edge was a lot of rope. He unravelled it carefully and it turned itself into a perfectly made rope ladder, attached to the inside of the bump with iron staples.

They dangled it through the hole and it was exactly right, the last rung reaching the platform.

"Let's take the bag in with us," said Widgie. "Then we can have our sandwiches."

They bundled the shovel and the torch and thermos into the plastic bag and then Widgie went first, carrying it.

"You wait till I'm down, Jen."

It wasn't as easy as he'd thought, going down a rope ladder. His feet kept shooting away from underneath him so that he thought he would end up on his back. Once one of the sandwiches slid out of the bag and landed with a thump on the platform, but eventually he got his feet on solid ground and then he was able to hold the rope steady for Jen.

Now that they were actually on the station instead of looking at it from above it was even more exciting, particularly the size of everything, which was in between the little railways they'd been on at the seaside, and the real thing. When they went into the Waiting Room their heads just got through the door and the ceiling was only about two feet above their heads. It had a large polished table in the middle and long wooden benches along the sides and even a fireplace, neatly laid with wood and paper but not alight.

"Just like a Waiting Room—cold," said Jen, shivering. "Let's go and see the Booking Office."

There wasn't much to see there, so they went through a side-door into the office part and looked at the ticket-rack.

LONG SHAFT—GOSPEL OAK. CHEAP DAY RETURN
LONG SHAFT—ANGEL BASIN. SINGLE
LONG SHAFT—EASTERN LINE. UNLIMITED
  TRAVEL

"It's all very well organized." Widgie peered through the window. "Let's go over the footbridge to the other side—there's a Refreshment Room there."

It was rather a grand Refreshment Room with marble-topped tables and cane chairs and a beautiful silver tea-urn. On one of the tables there was a half-eaten bun and a cup of cold tea, and a jacket hung over the back of the chair.

They looked at each other in silence, and then went outside rather quickly to look at the engine.

"It's a 2-4-0 Precedent class, I think," said Widgie, "but it's painted dark-red, which it shouldn't be."

"It's very old-fashioned looking."

"Of course it is," said Widgie scornfully. "It's a very old-fashioned class, the Precedent."

"N.L.R." said Jen thoughtfully.

"North London Railway, I suppose." Widgie felt impatient—he had been feeling quite hungry since looking into the Refreshment Room—"Let's go and get our sandwiches."

He rescued the one that had dropped out of the bag, and

then they sat themselves on the edge of the platform and dangled their legs over the track while they ate them.

"It's not really dark at all," said Jen, looking round. "I wonder where the light comes from?"

"Some of it comes from up the line." Widgie pointed. "Look, it's quite bright where the track bends round to the left."

Jen peered up at the roof of the tunnel.

"Some comes from up there, too. There's a sort of opening. Look—there's another higher up."

"They must be ventilation shafts," said Widgie, sniffing. "It doesn't smell really stuffy." He thought a minute. "That means they come out somewhere in the real world—I wonder where. I say, Jen, we could look for them when we get back."

"I love all the *little* things," said Jen. "Like the real glass in the windows and all the signs being so beautifully written."

"It's very clean and tidy. I wonder who looks after it?"

"I wonder who *built* it—it must have been a long while ago because everything's so old-fashioned; and it's been used a lot too—it's all tidy but it's pretty well worn."

"Open the thermos," said Widgie, "I'm dying for some tea."

He poured himself a cup, and wandered across the track to the engine. "Shall I climb into the cab?"

"I don't see why not, but for goodness sake don't pull anything or it might go."

Widgie put his foot on the iron step and hauled himself up.

"The fire-door's open and it's full of wood and coal, but it's not alight."

"Of course it's not, you ass, otherwise it'd be smoking."

"Hey; come up, Jen; let's be engine-drivers."

"No—I want to have a look up the track. Be careful with that engine—I don't want to be run down."

She slid off the platform and began wandering up the

lines, eating her ham sandwich. Widgie watched her through the little window at the side of the cab.

"I can see a bit of sky through one of the shafts," she shouted, pointing upwards. "It's an awfully long way up."

She wandered off again, peering from side to side as she went. When she got up to the bend, Widgie saw her silhouette against the light. She did a little skip, gave him a wave and then ran out of sight.

3

The Railwaymen

Widgie turned back to his controls. He had never been in an engine cab before but he felt sure this must be a replica of the real thing. There were gauges and dials and miles of complicated piping, and everything was labelled with neat metal plates: REGULATOR; STEAM BRAKE; REVERSING GEAR; WATER GAUGES, they said. In spite of Jen's warning, Widgie couldn't help turning some of them to see if they worked—after all the train couldn't go anywhere without a fire—and they did; in fact, everything was so well-oiled that moving them became a pleasure.

Then he saw a handle near the roof of the cab labelled WHISTLE, and who could resist that, so he pulled it as hard as he could. It let off such an appalling shriek that Widgie fell backwards onto the edge of the tender. "Ow," he said, getting his balance again and rubbing his bottom. "What a row."

He climbed down onto the track and examined the engine more carefully. It was painted dark red with all the outlines etched in bright gold, and it looked most handsome. It had a number on the side of the cab: 791, and over the wheel-cover was its name, also in bright gold: THE FLYING BLOGGER. Widgie giggled—what a silly name for an engine. It had only one connecting-rod each side—altogether a fairly basic job, Widgie thought. In front, as well as the bumpers and coupling-gear, it had three brackets holding oil-lamps with reflectors inside, and across the front of the boiler was written in black, raised letters: NORTH LONDON

LINE—RETURN TO LONG SHAFT.

Widgie climbed onto the platform and stood back to admire the whole effect—very fine, he thought—and then he walked farther back to look at the trucks. They were all sizes, and some had E.L. written on the sides, and some N.L.R. and some W.L. and they were all empty, even the ones with tarpaulin over them, because Widgie lifted the sides to have a look.

He had just got to the Guard's Van and was about to climb inside it, when he quite suddenly had a funny feeling come over him that left him tingling all over. He stopped, one foot on the bottom step of the van, and tried to place it. It had been hiding at the back of his mind for quite a long while, he realized, but for some reason it now stood up and asked to be noticed.

It's something to do with the quietness, thought Widgie. Everything's too quiet—it's as if it's all waiting for something.

He hadn't noticed it when Jen was there because they'd been clattering about; but now it seemed not just an absence of noise but rather a sort of silent shouting. It was like waking up in the middle of the night with a noise in your ears.

He peered carefully all around, but everything was as it was.

I must look more carefully, he thought, and not just at the obvious things. For some reason he didn't want to move or make a noise, so he just turned his head round this way and that.

The station—yes, he'd seen that. Perhaps behind the station?

He turned right round and peered into the gloom, and then he saw the dark openings. Quite a lot of them. They led off at intervals along the tunnel, and he had the impression that they were deep.

He wanted to go over and have a look at them, but something said, "Don't." He felt he mustn't disturb anything for the moment.

With a great effort he took his foot off the step of the Guard's Van and tiptoed to the back of the train. There was nothing there except the tunnel disappearing backwards. Above him was a big hole with daylight coming through it, but he couldn't see the sky as Jen had. Perhaps it was curved.

This is silly, he thought. And then quite suddenly he knew what it was.

I'm being watched. I'm being watched by lots of people and that's why it seems so quiet.

He thought about this for a minute to get over the shock, and then he pulled himself together and became the real Widgie again.

He strode back to the engine, deliberately making as much noise as he could, and when he'd got there he looked all around, put his hands on his hips and shouted:

"Hallo everyone—where are you?"

The answer came immediately—rough and very loud.

"Alright—handle 'im, men."

There was a rush of feet from behind, and before he could even turn round he felt his legs dragged from under him and his arms pinioned. He fell backwards with a crash and hit his head on the platform.

"Ow. Stop it."

People were sitting on his chest now, and holding down his legs and arms. "Jen," roared Widgie in a fury.

"That'll do you no good," said the voice.

"Jen!" roared Widgie again.

"Shut yer mouth," said the voice. Widgie tried to turn his head in its direction and he saw a figure climbing down the rope ladder.

I must get my arms free, thought Widgie, and then he remembered a trick he had often used in the playground at school. He let his whole body go limp and as he did so he felt everyone's grip relax a little. Then he made his big effort, and jerked suddenly upwards. He felt rather than saw the people falling off him, and then he twisted round and managed to get on his hands and knees. He was able to look up now, and the first thing he saw were dozens more people rushing over the footbridge from the other platform. They were all waving pickaxes and shovels.

"Alright," he shouted. "Pax—I surrender."

He hated saying it, but there seemed to be no alternative.

"Get off 'im but guard 'im," said the man from the rope ladder as he reached the ground and pushed his way through the crowd. He stood in front of Widgie and looked down at him.

"Get up," he said with great authority.

Widgie clambered to his feet awkwardly and stood there staring around, getting his breath back and brushing muck off his trousers.

"What's the matter?" he said. "I haven't done anything wrong."

"Ho, you 'aven't, 'aven't you?"

The man was about the same height as Widgie but fully grown—he badly needed a shave. He was wearing a shovel hat, trousers tied with string just below the knee and big boots, and his face was strong, white and lined with coal-dust.

"Well I says you 'ave, so there, and so does we all," he said, striking an attitude.

Voices were raised, at first in a mumble, but getting louder.

"Ay, so do we all. That's what we all says."

Widgie looked round indignantly at the crowd—there must have been at least two hundred of them, all about his size and all dressed with the same shovel hats and boots. The man watched him carefully.

"See? We all agrees, and I'll tell you why. 'Cos this is Private Property and you're trespassing—*that's* what you've done wrong."

Widgie breathed hard and tried to control his temper.

"Well, it doesn't *say* it's Private Property so how should I know?"

"By using your nut, young fellow, that's 'ow. You've been prying, and don't tell me you didn't know it. Prying into our secrets."

"Then why didn't you stop me? I bet you saw me all the time."

"*Saw* you, yes. Of course we *saw* you, but we respect people's privacy same as you oughter respect people's privacy. Besides, we couldn't."

Widgie saw that this argument could go on for a long time, so he decided to shift ground a bit.

"Anyway, I'm not going to say another word till you go and fetch Jen."

"Jen? 'Oo's Jen?"

"My sister, that's who Jen is."

"Well if Jen's the girl that went up the line just now, I can tell you here and now you'll never get *her* back. Canal Folk'll have her by now and there ain't no question about it."

Widgie was aghast.

"What *do* you mean—never get her back? And what do you mean—Canal Folk. Who are they and who are you for that matter?"

The man stuck his thumbs in his belt with great satisfaction.

"We're the Railwaymen and Canal Folk be Canal Folk and never the twain shall meet, as is being said Above. Leastways, not without a bust-up. But I'll tell you this, young feller, and I'll tell you for nothing—*we're* the ones what's going to win. Ho, yes; ain't no two ways about it. We'll win if it takes another hundred years."

There was a low rumble of approval from all sides, and some banged their shovels and pickaxes on the ground.

Widgie could hardly see a glimmer of sense or reason in all this, but he realized that he must find out more about these very odd people if he was going to get Jen back.

"Look here," he said. "What's your name?"

"Bloggs and what's yours?"

"Widgie," said Widgie, "And Jen's my sister as I said, and I'm jolly well going to find her."

"Easy to say: 'going to find 'er.' Easy to say Mr Widgie, but if I might make so bold as to ask, 'ow was you proposing thus to do, eh Mr Widgie? Eh?" He leant forward suddenly and put his face right up against Widgie's.

"Well, I suppose if I went up the line like Jen did, these Canal Folk or whatever-they're-called will get me too and then I expect I'll find her."

Bloggs drew back and his voice was suddenly very sharp indeed.

"Hold 'ard, Mr Widgie. Not so fast, *if* you please. You, Mr Widgie, is with *us*. Not to put too fine a point on it, you're our prisoner. You does what we say and you goes where we say you goes, and nowhere else. Do I make myself clear, Mr Widgie? 'Cos I wouldn't wish you to misunderstand me on this little point."

Widgie felt absolutely at a loss.

"But why?" he said desperately. "What have I *done*? I've not harmed you at all and nor do I wish to and all you do is to poke pickaxes at me and say I'm your prisoner. It's just not fair."

Bloggs spat scornfully on the floor.

"Weren't doing no 'arm! That's a fine one. You poked about our Pit, didn't you? You found our key, didn't you? You found *us*, didn't you? Blinking well *found* us. No *'arm*!

"No, me lad, we're not letting *you* go, not for a month of Sundays and nor will them Canallers let your sister go if they've got any sense. Which I must say they often don't 'ave," he added as an afterthought.

"Well if they often don't have, p'raps they *will* let her go and then you'll look silly because she'll go to the police if she can't find me and *then* you'll be in trouble."

Bloggs regarded him thoughtfully.

"You're too smart by 'arfs you are," he said in a most unfriendly way.

He struck an attitude indicating thought, and the Railwaymen transferred their attention from Widgie to Bloggs, looking at him expectantly.

Widgie even wondered if he should take advantage of the moment to make a bolt for it, but he had a feeling he wouldn't get very far, so he contented himself with pushing some of the pickaxes a bit farther away.

After about a minute, Bloggs shook himself like a dog and looked around.

"Bodger!" he roared.

A raffish-looking Railwayman with a huge red beard and bright blue eyes—Widgie had never seen eyes so blue—pushed his way forward.

"Ay Bloggs—here I be, all present and correct."

Bloggs raised his voice so that all could hear and spoke in an oddly ponderous way.

"I 'ave thought, Bodger, and me thoughts are as follows. Here we have this Widgie-boy what we're not going to let go—ho, no. And up the line is his sister who them Canallers won't let go, neither. No doubts there. Now where d'ye think them Canallers are going to take the Widgie-boy's sister? Eh Bodger? Where?"

"If you was to ask me Bloggs, which you 'ave, I'd say they'd take 'er to Beasley's Arches, that's what I'd say."

"Ho. You would, would you Bodger? Well so would I, and me next thought is—I wouldn't mind fetching this Widgie-boy's sister and bringing her back 'ere, thus having the both of 'em. *That* would be somewhat to me liking—having the both of 'em. *That* might show them Canal Folk who's boss and who's not, eh Bodger?"

"Ay Bloggs, you could be right."

"Well, Bodger, just supposing I *am* right, for a minute,

what does this 'appy combination of circumstance suggest
to me next, Bodger? I'll tell you, Bodger—it suggests to me
that we go the whole hog and take the Arches back. How's
that for a thought, eh? *Take back Beasley's Arches.*"

There was a silence.

Bodger looked at his boots and then up at the roof, and
then round at the Railwaymen and then back at Bloggs.
Then he fumbled in his pockets and found an old cob pipe
and a tinder-box. He looked round in an absent-minded
way and someone handed him a taper, and when he had the
pipe alight, he puffed at it reflectively.

"Canallers have had Beasley's these last fifty year as I
recollect."

"Ay Bodger."

"They've 'ad us Long Shafters blocked up 'ere for three,
give or take."

"Ay Bodger."

"You want us Long Shafters to take the Arches alone?"

"We can't mobilize the whole North London system if
we're blocked up, can we, Bodger? Ay, alone."

"We've had no spies out these eight month, Bloggs.
There's no knowing what them Canallers 'ave done to our
tracks."

"Ay Bodger, true enough."

"They'll have made traps, Bloggs. Traps right up the line.
Ambushes at every crossing, Bloggs, and the first crossing
is just round that bend there, Bloggs—just past the Long
Shaft."

"Ay."

"They'll flood Fleet River when they hear us coming,
Bloggs."

"Then we'll have to get over Fleet first, won't we Bodger."

"Ay Bloggs. We *would* 'ave to if we was to take the
Arches."

Bodger changed his stance as he changed his argument.
He wagged his pipe at Bloggs.

"And why does you want this Jen-girl so bad, Bloggs?"

"I don't want 'er so bad as I want them Arches, and you know that, Bodger. But if we have *both* the Above-grounders, we can make bargains, Bodger. Bargains you can't even think of, Bodger. It's the first time it's happened, Bodger, and it's a mortal danger to us all. Them that keeps 'em has the power and power's what we want—for the Railway *and* for Long Shaft."

There was a long silence while Bodger looked at his boots and puffed at his pipe; it went on so long that Widgie thought it would never end. Someone shuffled their feet, a shovel scraped on the platform.

At last Bodger looked around him and then up at Bloggs.

"I don't 'ave no hobjections, Bloggs," he said.

Bloggs stuck his thumbs in his belt.

"You heard that, men? We 'ave deliberated and we 'ave decided. What is it we 'ave so decided?"

There was a sudden shout.

"To take Beasley's. 'Ooray, 'ooray. Take Beasley's and whack 'em."

Bloggs waved his arms for quiet.

"Then listen to me, men, and then get on with it—I don't want any mucking like last time.

"First we get the train ready—fire lit Mr Stoker, and all trim. I want fifteen men in each truck, so that means we couple up four more. Then I want the Passenger Coach at the back, but in front of the Guard's Van, and I want fifty men in that.

"Now the first attack will come from Long Shaft just round the bend, but if they ain't mucked up the bridge I shall steam right through. I can't go on full steam on account of not knowing about the bridge, and I ain't going to wreck the *Flying Blogger* not for no-one. So we'll take it steady and if they starts clambering aboard, ye'll know what to do.

"But whichever way it is, they'll know we're coming and

they'll know there's a lot of us. They'll get news down the Canals and they'll get it down fast—I don't know how they does it but they does it. They won't know our route, but they'll know we 'ave to cross the Fleet, and like Bodger says, they'll flood it.

"What Bodger didn't say though, and I does, is this—it takes best part of an hour to flood Fleet and if I can't get over Fleet in an hour I'll eat my shovel hat, as is said. I aim for quickest route—that is Gospel Oak and Savernake—but if tracks are mucked up we might 'ave to go anywheres on the system to get through. But get through we will or my name's not Bloggs and my engine's not the *Flying Blogger*. Do I make myself clear?"

"Ay Bloggs—clear enough" came a voice, grimly.

"Right. Now—Quirker—where are you, Quirker?"

Quirker was bow-legged and skinny and he walked with his head and shoulders thrust forward so that he always seemed to be looking at the ground.

"Speaking Bloggs," he muttered at the floor.

"Lock this Widgie-boy in the Great Cellar and choose yourself three more to guard him. I don't want 'im left alone day or night."

"I 'ave a slight hobjection," said Bodger quickly.

Bloggs looked at him sharply. "Ay?"

"I be not entirely for that we lock up this 'ere Widgie-boy."

"Ho, and why not Bodger?"

"On account of 'is astonishing pryingness, that's why not. I wouldn't feel easy in me mind with him left 'ere, even if we left twenty men to guard him."

"Take him with us Bodger and he could sabotage all our plans if he had a mind to."

Widgie suddenly got cross at being talked about. He stepped forward between Bloggs and Bodger and looked Bloggs straight in the eye.

"Look here—Jen's *my* sister and we're going to try to

find her and bring her back here, and that's all that concerns me. But if we have to have a fight to get her—well, I'm pretty strong and I bet I'm as good a fighter as any of your Railwaymen. I think you should be grateful I'm here instead of treating me like a child and locking me up in the cellar. There."

He stopped, having run out of breath, and Bloggs gave him a hard look for what seemed a long while.

"Alright Bodger, I be with you. Put 'im in Truck Three and guard 'im, and you'll be answerable to me if he gets out. When it comes to a fight, watch him and tell me how he does.

"Now can we get down to business? Couple up the trucks, men—we shall need five extra now. Mister Stoker? Ah, there ye are—get the fires lit. Bring the great Western tender from the sheds and break me enough coal to damp down if needed. Light the lamps, men, and get the tarpaulins stripped back but keep 'em with us. Briggs—we shall need more water in the boiler—throw the hose into the tankhole and fill her up as high as you can. Brossel; fill the oil-cups to the pistons, Brossel, and not so meanly as last time. Bostock; get the wheels tapped and oiled, and I mean well oiled so she don't clatter and drag like a dray. We need lights, men. Get lights to check the couplings, and fix up the big reflector in front. Mister Guard, you check we get the numbers right in the trucks, and I want all blinds down in the Big Coach. Make sure they get a crowbar each and don't move till they gets the Whistle."

The men were on the move now, running from tunnels to train and station to engine to get all done, while Bloggs strode from end to end, eyes flashing with determination.

"Get it done right and thorough, men; we're going to add a chapter to the Legends tonight and I 'ave a mind to put a name to it—When the Railway rode back and broke the Arches at Beasley's."

4

The Canal Folk

When Jen said she was going to have a look up the track, what she really meant was, "I'm going to see where that light comes from." For she was absolutely fed-up with the semi-darkness and gloom and was dying to see some sun again. It was quite fun, all the same, peering up at the ventilation shafts and down the side-tunnels, but when she got to the bend itself and was faced with losing sight of Widgie and the station she had a moment of panic.

"Oh don't be silly," she said to herself crossly. "Look at that lovely daylight," and she gave a little skip of anticipation and ran towards it.

It was much farther than she thought, but as the tunnel got lighter and lighter she stopped feeling nervous and began enjoying herself again. There didn't seem to be so many side-tunnels now, and as the light ahead got brighter so did the two tracks get wider apart and the tunnel bigger, until at last she caught a glimpse of blue sky.

Hooray—I'll go and get Widgie, she thought, but a few steps further on "Oh," she cried in dismay. For she wasn't really in the open-air at all; she was only in a very deep cutting lined with bricks like the tunnel but with no roof. Certainly if she looked up she could see some sky, but it was almost worse than *not* seeing it if she couldn't get out to it.

Surely there must be *some* way up. She began looking round the walls of the cutting for ladders or perhaps even toeholds in the brickwork, but there was nothing. Oh what idiots they were whoever built this. She leant her head backwards and looked up at the opening. The walls of the cutting, which were about thirty feet apart at the base, gradually narrowed as they went up, until at the top there was only about five feet between them, so little in fact that the leaves and branches of the bushes growing up there met right across.

Jen tried to work out where it could be, so that she and Widgie could go and visit it later, but she couldn't imagine where anyone would be allowed to put such a dangerous hole in the ground. We must tell the police or something— it's just not safe. Someone else must have had the same idea, she decided, for although the cutting itself was really quite long—perhaps two hundred feet—most of the openings at the top had been blocked up at some time, leaving only five separate gaps of perhaps ten feet each through which one could see the sky. She walked on a little way, holding her nose up and sniffing what air managed to find its way down to her, and then, just as she was thinking 'Well that wasn't much fun—it was better back at the station,' she saw the bridge.

It was right at the end of the cutting where the tunnel became a tunnel again and it was for the railway track to go over something even lower in the ground. It looked very impressive because although it wasn't very big it was beautifully made and proportioned. The two tracks converged into one just before it so that it didn't have to be too wide, and its sides were curved and rather high for its width.

Jen began to trot towards it to see what it went over, and when she got there she peered down eagerly, thinking to see another railway track, perhaps. She certainly wasn't prepared to see her own reflection looking up at her.

"It's a river," she exclaimed, and then, seeing its tidy brick sides, "No, it's a canal." She peered along it and got the surprise of her life. "A canal with a boat in it I mean."

She hadn't seen it at first, because part of it went under

the bridge; in fact, it was so long and narrow that its bows disappeared into the canal tunnel to her left. Jen decided that it was a discovery with great possibilities, not least because the canal had a tunnel all of its own and was quite independent, so it seemed, of the railway system.

The boat itself had a high Z-shaped tiller at the back painted in red and green stripes and then a sort of platform for the boatman to stand on. Then came a cabin painted green and covered with carefully painted pictures of flowers and castles in red and yellow, and half-way along its sides it had a pair of double doors made of polished wood.

Jen walked over the tracks to the left of the bridge to see them better, and she decided that the front part of the cabin after the doors must be an engine-room, because it had a tall, slender funnel in front of it from which a little blue smoke curled gently. The rest of the boat was quite empty—a long hold about three feet deep for cargoes to be stored.

Jen was entranced by it all; she stood back and looked at it with deep admiration. "I wonder what it's called," she said to herself out loud.

"It's called the *Blisterlee*," said a rather cracked, thin voice.

Jen gave a scream of fright and then felt ashamed of herself.

"I'm so sorry—I didn't mean to scream but you gave me such a surprise. I didn't think there was anyone down here apart from us."

She was still looking for the voice, which had seemed to come from the boat although there was no-one to be—oh, yes there was. He was quite a small man and he was coming out of the polished door.

"Hullo—you're not a Railwayman," he said, staring very hard at Jen while she stared equally hard back at him.

He was wearing a red and white striped jersey with a low, round neck, tattered old grey flannels and a cloth cap that had once been green but was now largely black grease. He was very thin and rangy of body and his face was all nose—a thin, pointed one. He kept tugging at a red and white kerchief that was knotted round his throat, while his eyes flickered everywhere at once—at Jen, at the boat, up at the sunlight and back to Jen.

"No," said Jen, not knowing what on earth he was talking about—Railwaymen?—"I'm Jen, and my brother and I were having a look at the station."

He looked at her, puzzled, and his eyes flickered more than ever.

"Were you?" His voice was absent-minded, as though he was thinking of something else very hard. "Well, well—and your, um, brother's here as well, is he? Goodness me, fancy that, well I'll be—and where's your brother now then, I wonder? Where's, um, what did you say his name was?"

"I didn't, but he's called Widgie."

"That's right, Widgie. Nice name, um, Widgie," he rolled it round his mouth and tasted it. "And where's your, um, where's Widgie now?"

"He's up at the station looking at the engine-cab, or at any rate that's where he was when I left him."

"*Is* he now? Goodness me, fancy that; well I'll be—well that's that, I suppose. What a pity. Nice boy too I shouldn't wonder—great pity."

"What *do* you mean?" Jen felt distinctly uneasy.

"Nothing, me dear, nothing at all, nothing at—and I s'pose *you* haven't seen the Railwaymen?" He looked sharply at her for at least five seconds.

"I don't know *what* you're talking about. You're the only person we've seen."

He flickered around vaguely, as if he was trying to make up his mind about something.

"Yes, well, I s'pose that's a possibility. Just about a possibility."

Jen was beginning to feel quite uncomfortable with this

flickering man with the nose, and also she was feeling very Widgieless, so she said in the sort of voice her school-teacher used, "Well, I'm delighted to have met you, but I must get back to Widgie now and see how he's getting on."

The little man suddenly stopped being vague and puzzled, and leapt to life.

"Oh, no, you mustn't do that." He jumped from the barge onto the track-side next to Jen. "No, no you really mustn't go yet, me dear; you must wait here a moment—no don't try to run away—I'm only *holding* your arm in a friendly way like—just let me think a moment—*don't push me*—yes, that's it, just stay still awhile—you see, me dear, the trouble is I'm affeared that you may be a...er...a... SPY," and he shouted out the word SPY at the top of his voice.

"SPY ... SPY ..." came an answering shout from the bushes above, and down from them came a rope, and then another, and then lots more, all curling down the brick sides of the cutting like very long black snakes. Jen looked up panic-stricken and saw a lot of replicas of the boatman coming down them very fast all shouting "SPY, SPY" in high, cracked voices.

She had no idea what was going on but she knew that she must get away at once, so she gave the boatman a very hard push in the chest, snatched away her arm and began running like mad for the station. She could hear him shouting "Catch 'er, catch 'er," and she could hear feet pounding after her as the men got to the ground—more and more of them every second. "*Catch* the Spy, *catch* the Spy," they were shouting.

Jen felt pretty sure she was gaining on them, because she was running absolutely full-pelt and when she did this she was considered to be fast. Also the mouth of the tunnel was getting nearer and nearer, and for some reason she knew she would be safe once she was in it. Then her left foot caught one of the sleepers and she stumbled—not much, but just enough to slow her down and for a man to grab her arm and another to catch hold of one of her feet. She didn't even come down with a crash, because by then they were all around her, hoisting her off her legs and carrying her, kicking and struggling, back to the canal.

"Widgie!" she shouted. "Widgie!"

"Shut yer trap," and someone tied a big handkerchief round her mouth.

"You'll not be hurt if you stop struggling like a young barge-pony."

"Get another man on that leg there."

She didn't stop struggling and fighting, but all she could say now was "Mmmm."

Then she thought: Thank goodness—they're putting me down, but as she was being lowered, suddenly the ground wasn't there any more.

Help, I do believe they're going to drown me. She saw the brick sides of the canal and felt herself being passed like a sack of coal from one group to another; so she struggled even harder and managed to get one leg free, and she kicked out with it. She heard a splash as someone went over into the water and this was followed by much spluttering and swearing.

"Tie her up and put her in the bows," shouted a voice. "She be too big and wild for me."

And then Jen realized that they were bundling her into the barge. They managed to grab her leg back and then they lumped her to the front and sat on her while two of them bound her arms and legs with rope. They propped her up against the gunwales and stood round regarding her.

"She be a kid from up there, Blister," and one of them jerked a thumb upwards.

"Mmmm," said Jen.

"She says as her brother's down at the station."

"Wouldn't give much for his chances—not with that Bloggs in charge."

"Mmmm."

"What shall we do with 'er?"

"Better take her to the Captain, I s'pose."

"What, all the way to Beasley's? Take us best part of an hour."

"Well, we can't leave her here."

"Tell you what—take 'er to Shipley's Basin and then one of the regulars can take her rest of the way."

"Ay—might just do that."

Jen was by now thoroughly frightened, particularly when she heard the bit about Widgie, but she was also nearly choking on her gag and that was a more immediate worry. She tried chewing it.

"How'd she get down 'ere, anyways? They never have before."

"Wasn't there a once when someone did? Something about it in the Legends."

"Never believed it, meself."

"Well there y'are—p'raps you will now."

"What'll Captain do with her—can't let her get back up there again and blow the gaff."

"What'll Bloggs do with her brother?"

"Bloggs won't let 'im go. He may be only a Railwayman but he's not that stoopid."

"We ought to have the brother as well. That way we know where we stand."

"If Bloggs knows she's 'ere, I bet he tries to get 'er."

"Ay, better get 'er off to Beasley's if you ask me—he'll never get 'er there. Hey listen—what's that?"

"What's what?"

"Sshh"—a hand was held up for silence and it became so quiet that Jen could hear herself chewing at the gag. She stopped and her eyes swivelled round to see what was wrong. No-one was moving and it seemed as if they all had their heads cocked on one side.

Then from the railway-tunnel she heard, they all heard, a

47

distinct and solitary, *Chuff*.

Oh Widgie, you *ass*, she thought. You haven't started the engine up?

There was a heavy clank.

"They're coming," someone whispered.

"They wouldn't dare."

Chuff, chuff.

"They're going to try a break-out."

"After three year? Never."

"Blinking well are. Listen."

They stood still and silent. Jen could hear the rustle of the bushes up above.

There was a distant hiss of steam being released and more clanking. No-one moved or spoke, and then Blister stamped his foot with sudden decision.

"Right. That's it. They're on the move. We'll whack 'em right here in Long Shaft. Up the ropes, all of you. Fillbreach and Reech come with me and we'll get the girl away and down to Beasley's.

"Jumper—winch that bridge back and stay at your post and hold that winch till they kills you. We'll make this a battle for the Legends."

"Ay, ay Blister."

"We'll not let ye down, Blister."

"Up ropes all."

Jen watched as best she could in her position as they all swarmed up the ropes, not as she had first thought to the bushes, but to a long, narrow brick balcony that ran the whole length of the cutting. How odd, she thought. I didn't see it before.

Jumper had unpadlocked the winch, and as he turned it, the bridge slowly lumbered round until it stood horizontal to the canal. Blister was already at the tiller of the *Blisterlee* and Fillbreach and Reech were casting off the mooring ropes.

"Which way will ye take, Blister?"

"Shipley's Basin?"

"No, you fool—not now. Quickest route now, through Low Tunnel."

At last Jenny managed to work her gag down to her chin. What blessed relief as she swallowed. "What about Widgie?" she shouted—she couldn't think of anything else to say.

"Quiet girl," said Reech. "Otherwise there's plenty more kerchiefs where that one came from."

The boat slipped gently into the tunnel. Poor Mum— she'll get so worried, thought Jen.

Jumper padlocked the winch again and hid himself behind it.

The wash from the boat lapped against the sides of the canal and an uneasy peace reigned.

From the station came a whistle. Again silence. Jumper moved a little to avoid cramp. The canal was still again and Jumper could feel the quietness waiting with him. Suddenly he lifted his head, for he had heard the noise he dreaded.

Chuff.

Chuff, chuff, chuff, chuff.

With a great and distant clanking a train gathered speed, and as he heard it getting louder and nearer, Jumper slid down onto his knees and began saying his prayers.

INTERLUDE I

284 Cranley Gardens,
Muswell Hill

When Jen and Widgie didn't come home for lunch, their mother didn't worry. They had their tea and sandwiches and during the school holidays they often stayed out all day. She went and looked at their bedrooms to see if they'd tidied them properly and really they weren't too bad. She decided to take advantage of their no doubt short-lived tidiness to hoover them, and in doing so she discovered quite a lot of things that had been shoved under the beds. She gave a deliberately loud sigh, and piled them all in the centre of each room to show that she was not to be fooled that easily.

Then she went down to the shops for some new hoover bags, and also bought a Dundee cake for tea to prove that she wasn't all mean.

It was four o'clock when she got back, so she rushed around making egg and cucumber sandwiches, which for some reason they liked, and she thought, I won't make tea till they get back—they're bound to be late. But by a quarter to five she had got tired of waiting, so she made a pot for herself and helped herself to some of the Dundee cake.

By half past five, she began going to the door to look up and down the road, and at six o'clock, when her husband got home, she was feeling quite panicky and near to tears. "They *always* come home for tea," she said.

Mr Widgeon saw the point of this, so they both went out to look and even walked down to the corner of the street.

50

He put his arm round her and said, "Really darling, I'm sure they're O.K. I'll give them hell when they get back."

But by seven they still weren't, and the Widgeons were sitting in the kitchen drinking too much tea and trying to read the evening papers. Eventually Mr Widgeon got up and said, "Well, I don't want to bother them, because I'm sure they're alright really, but p'raps I'd better ring the police."

Mrs Widgeon nodded miserably, because ringing the police meant that there really *was* something wrong.

So he went into the hall and she could hear him saying, "Anyway, although I'm sure it's alright, it *is* half past seven —yes, my wife heard them say something about going down the embankment onto the old railway lines. What? Yes, just by the old station. Well, that's most kind—I'll meet you up there. Sorry? Oh, stay by the phone. Alright, if you think that's better. Yes. Thank you *very* much—sorry to be a nuisance."

"They're going to have a look," he said, coming back into the kitchen.

Mrs Widgeon was really crying now. "Oh dear, can't we go with them?"

"They say to stay by the phone, so I suppose we'd better," and he put his arm round her again.

Suddenly she sat up with a jolt. "There aren't any trains up there still, are there?"

"Of course not; there aren't even any rails."

"Well, if they haven't been run over, where can they have got to? I know—they've got lost in a tunnel."

"You don't get *lost* in tunnels, darling. You just go in one end and come out the other."

"Not if you've got that Widgie with you, you don't."

5

Long Shaft

Oh, what a lurching and a bumping Widgie got as the train gathered speed. He clung hard to both sides of the truck and tried not to choke as the smoke from the engine got into his throat.

Bodger, who seemed quite unaffected by all this, waved his shovel warningly at Widgie.

"Now don't you forget whose side you're on, Widgie-boy. When it comes to a fight, you fight with *us* because we're the ones what's fetching your sister. Understood? I shall 'ave me eye on you like Bloggs said, and I don't want any mucking about."

Widgie wanted to say 'In that case why don't you give me a shovel to fight *with*,' but just at that moment the train took the bend in the track and Widgie lost his balance and rolled over onto his back.

Ouch.

As he picked himself up, he noticed the tunnel getting lighter, so he leant out of the truck and watched a pinpoint of light ahead getting bigger and bigger. Soon he could see Bodger quite clearly and then suddenly it was broad daylight. Widgie automatically looked above him and he saw the blue sky through the overhanging bushes of Long Shaft.

"Ah, that's better"—he breathed deeply, but before he could really enjoy it there was a dreadful roar of braking from the engine and then a deafening clatter as, one after the other, the trucks banged into each other. This time *everyone* was thrown off their feet, even Bodger, and from up in the engine cab there came a great and angry shout from Bloggs.

"The Bridge is turned—they've winched back the Bridge. Stand ready, men; there's like to be a fight," and before the Railwaymen could even pick themselves up, he had got down from the engine and was striding angrily over to the winch in the corner.

"The Bridge, the Bridge!" shouted the Railwaymen, scrambling out of their trucks, and from high above they heard the thin answer; "The Canal, the Canal!" and half-a-hundred ropes slapped down from the balcony at the top of Long Shaft and a hundred Canallers began swarming down them.

Bloggs looked up. "Pick 'em off as they land men—they won't stand a chance," and he strode on to the winch. When he was only two feet away from it, Jumper stepped from the shadows and barred his way.

"Over my dead body, Bloggs."

Bloggs stopped and stared at this piece of rash impudence. He lifted his shovel and raised it high.

"So be it," he said grimly, and brought it crashing down.

Then Jumper jumped.

It was his speciality, perfected over the years, and he not only twisted out of the path of Bloggs' shovel but he gave him a sharp kick as he fell. The shovel hit the ground and Bloggs doubled up, winded.

Bodger and some of the Railwaymen saw it all happen and they rushed over in a fury, Widgie with them.

"Get back, ye fools," grunted Bloggs. "They'll be on you in a minute."

They looked back and saw the first Canallers landing and running at them, so they turned back to meet them.

But Widgie was still in the grip of his first thought, which had been to barge Jumper straight into the Canal, and he carried on like a little snub-nosed bullet. Jumper saw him coming out of the corner of his eye and jumped back, at the same time sticking out his foot. Widgie saw that he himself was just about to end up in the Canal, so he changed it from a soccer barge to a rugger tackle and they both crashed down together, Widgie on top.

Bloggs cast a quick but experienced eye over the battle and started breaking the padlock on the winch with his shovel.

The Railwaymen were getting the upper hand swiftly, by attacking the Canallers before they had a chance to get their feet on the ground. So successful were they that it looked as if the battle would become a massacre in no time.

Only when they heard the shout from above: "DROP", did they realize their danger, for the Canallers had held back their younger men till last, and now they were jumping from the ropes when they were still twenty feet or more from the ground. They knocked the Railwaymen flying as they landed, and then they began encircling them and separating them into isolated units. Bloggs looked up from the winch and saw the danger.

"Keep together, the Railway," he roared at the top of his voice. "Fight your way back to the trucks. Get your backs against the trucks."

He rushed forward to help, shouting ferociously, and managed to break up some of the Cannallers' encirclements. Gradually the Railwaymen established contact with each other again and then began to form a ragged line and retreat step by step to the trucks.

"The Canal," came the triumphant cry as the Canallers saw the retreat beginning.

"Regroup, Canallers, and smash 'em against their own trucks," shouted a voice, and the Canallers obeyed, and formed an advancing line, oars and billhooks held high and ready.

Once Widgie had Jumper underneath him where he could no longer jump, he found it quite easy to roll him over to the edge of the canal and give him a heavy shove.

Jumper gave a gasp and went under with a splash, and Widgie staggered up, surprised by the sudden quiet of the battle. Then he saw the grim line of Canallers advancing on the Railwaymen, and he saw them all as Jen's kidnappers and felt the fury of the Widgies rise up inside him. He flung himself at them shouting he knew not what.

"*Where's* Jen, *where's* Jen," he roared, rushing along the line of billhooks and oars and hitting out wildly at everyone at once. He had snapped the tension, and the Railwaymen blinked for a moment in astonishment and then lunged forward.

"Oh Gawd," said Bloggs, "exposing their rear again," and he dodged under the couplings to the far side of the trucks and ran up front to the engine. Just as he was hauling himself up into the cab, he caught sight of Jumper hauling himself out of the canal.

"Ho, I've got a use for you, me lad," he grunted, and he dragged Jumper to his feet and frogmarched him into the engine cab, where he tied him securely to the steam brake.

"You just dry off there for a moment, young feller-me-lad."

He looked down the line at the battle, trying to come to a decision. He hadn't intended to expose his full forces until he got to Beasley's, but this fight was harder than he'd thought. He turned back to the controls with a sigh, his mind made up, and the first thing he did was to pull the whistle as hard as he could and hold onto it.

The Canal Folk looked up in horror as the mighty shriek echoed down the Shaft, rolling from one wall to another and cutting through their ears like a knife. For a moment they hesitated, and one or two even crouched down on the ground, their hands over their heads; and in that moment there came a dreadful cry from the Passenger Coach at the back: "Death to the Canallers—glory to the Railway. Death and Glory!" and out charged Bloggs' fifty picked Railwaymen armed with crowbars.

The very savagery of their charge and the impact with which they hit the Canallers' flank caused it to bend and fall back, and carried them into the centre of the fight almost immediately, and the other Railwaymen took new courage and began forcing the Canallers back towards their ropes.

Bloggs stopped pulling the whistle, opened the regulator and put the engine into reverse gear. The *Flying Blogger* began to clank backwards and as she did so Bloggs opened the cylinder waste cocks and the battlefield was enveloped in a hiss of hot steam. The Railwaymen were used to this and paid little attention, but to the Canallers it was terrifying. Bloggs watched its effect with grim satisfaction, and then he drove forward again and sprayed the whole area again.

"Capture the engine—stop that Bloggs," shouted the Canallers, retreating fast, and a group at the Canal end of the battle managed to break through the Railwaymen and rush the engine-cab.

"Help," shouted Jumper, seeing his colleagues storming the cab, but they had eyes only for Bloggs.

"Shut it off, Bloggs, or we'll take you."

Bloggs grinned at them—as long as the train was in motion he knew they dare not touch him. He glanced up the line and saw the Canal about fifty yards ahead and he decided to risk it. With a great roar, he took his hands off the controls and hurled himself at them. There were seven of them and they were so taken by surprise that they had neither the time not the space to resist him. They fell back, one against the other, tried to get their balance, failed, and staggered down the steps onto the track.

Bloggs jumped back to his controls, put the blower on, shut the regulator and braked, just in time to bring the engine to a grinding halt only a couple of feet from the Canal.

He wiped his hands on some cotton waste and looked

at Jumper as if to say *'That's* the sort of man I am so you watch out.'

He leant out of the cab and surveyed the battlefield with satisfaction. Only half of the Canallers' total force were still fighting; the rest were either groping their way to the ropes or sitting by the tunnel wall nursing their wounds. Widgie he could see battling away with the reinforcements from the Coach. He had a black eye and was covered with grime, and every time he hit out he muttered "Jen" to himself.

It only took another five minutes for the Railwaymen to gain complete control and to start mopping-up operations and routing out stragglers who were hiding behind the trucks.

Bloggs got down from the cab and strode up and down issuing orders.

"Put all prisoners up the ropes—I don't care how damaged they are—send 'em back. Winch the bridge back—I've broken the padlock meself. When the Canallers are back up the top—burn every rope ye see. Get some lighted wood from the cab. When you've finished get back to ye trucks and rest—we've got a bigger fight than this when we get to Beasley's. Where's Smoker? Untie that man in the cab and stand guard over 'im with your shovel."

Bloggs strode back to the engine and Smoker, who was young and cheerful and full of the excitement of the battle, went ahead and untied Jumper. "No tricks now and ye'll be alright, but if ye tries anything ye'll get this 'ere shovel over your noddle."

Bloggs climbed into the cab and stood in front of a very sullen Jumper. He put his hands on his hips and looked at him very hard.

"Who be you?" said Bloggs.

"I be Jumper and I winched ye Bridge back and I was to defend it till death"—a touch of pride crept into his voice.

"Ho, were you?"

"Ay, and I would if that boy hadn't got me in the Canal, and if you be Bloggs, which I suspect, and if you be thinking of taking that train up the line, you can 'ave another think, 'cos Jumper's left some surprises for you right up the tracks as far as Reading Lock."

"Ho, 'ave you," said Bloggs, taken aback.

"Yes I 'ave, and you may 'ave won this blankety little fight, but you won't win the war, not in fifty year you won't, not after what Jumper's done."

"Ho, won't we?" said Bloggs, who suddenly saw that his best move was to keep quiet.

"No, you blankety-blank won't," said Jumper, getting quite excited. "'Cos there's booby traps right up your lines of a cunningness that'd make your hair stand on end. 'Cos you're trapped, you and your lot. You can rot in your blankety little station if you like, but you'll never get out again to make life a misery for all decent Canal Folk. That's what. . ."

He cocked his head on one side suddenly. From the Shaft had come the sound of crackling as the Railwaymen set fire to the ropes, one by one. Jumper realized that his lifeline was disappearing and his eyes flickered round at Smoker and Bloggs and he decided to risk it and jump again. In two long strides he was past them, giving each a strong shove, and with one huge jump he was not only down the cab steps but half-way to the ropes. Then he threw himself into the flames and disappeared.

"Get that Jumper," roared Bloggs as he got his balance back.

Smoker jumped from the cab and made a dive at Jumper's rope but it was burning too fast and he fell back, sucking his hands in pain.

Widgie heard the commotion and saw Smoker falling backwards with burnt hands. Without really thinking at all, but just as a reflex action, he ran at the rope and did his biggest jump. He felt a moment of scorching and then his hands were on solid rope, and with Jumper ahead and the flames below there was only one direction left to him.

He remembered his gym practice and really started working—arms up, legs up, arms up—until he realized that with the next arms up he might be able to reach one of Jumper's feet. He did the most colossal arms up and grabbed, and he had a foot in his hand which he decided to hold on to and they both crashed down together, Widgie underneath this time; bang!

Smoker left his hand-sucking and rushed over, dragging Jumper off Widgie and hauling him back to the cab.

"*Silly* Jumper," he said cheerfully.

Bloggs climbed down and went over to Widgie, who was very crumpled, scorched and forlorn. He lifted him to his feet and felt him all over.

"Nothing broken, young feller, so no yawping."

Widgie was, indeed, near tears as he examined himself anxiously. His head ached, he felt bruised all over and he was slightly scorched. Above all, he needed a bit of a fuss made of him, and he cheered up no end when he saw Bodger approaching with a steaming mug.

"Had a quick brew-up," said Bodger smugly. "Strong and hot with lots of sugar."

Widgie took it in both hands and slurped noisily—it was the best cup of tea he could remember, and a wave of gratitude and affection for tea and Bodger swept over him.

"Brought you a wheat-cake, too," said Bodger.

Widgie looked at it. "Thank you," he said.

It was the size of a small loaf but grey in colour, and as Widgie felt that he ought to build up his strength he began eating it—the taste was quite good, sour and milky.

"Where do you grow all this—wheat and tea and so forth?"

"In the Big Tillages of course. We got one of the best in the System at Long Shaft. We grows nearly everything, but turnips best—Long Shaft Turnips is famous all over. Even the Canallers used to buy 'em afore they blocked us up."

Widgie considered. "I didn't see any Big Tillages."

"There's lots you 'aven't seen yet, Widgie-boy. You 'ave to go down the Ramps to get to the Tillages."

"Well, who grows all these turnips and wheat and things? I bet you don't."

"I does me stint when the Womenfolk calls me before the Annual Wenching."

Widgie choked on some tea-leaves and decided that his curiosity about life below ground would have to wait, because just at that moment he caught sight of Bloggs frog-marching Jumper into the engine-cab for the second time, and he wanted to hear what he had to say.

"Right, Jumper. From now on there'll be no more jumping and no more arguments neither. You're going to speak when you're spoken to and answer up straight.

"First of all, where've they taken the Above-grounder girl? Beasley's, I suppose."

Jumper nodded miserably.

"Thought so. Now what about my route to Beasley's—you'll know about that won't you Jumper? *Won't you Jumper?*" suddenly threatening.

Jumper nodded.

"Tell me it, Jumper."

"Reservoir - Loop - via - Southern - Road - or - else - direct - to Whittington - cross - under - the - Eastern - Line - at - Great - North Road - under - the - Heath - to - Gospel - Oak - over - the - Fleet - and then - follow - the - London - Midland - line - past - Kentish - Town right - loop - through - Hawley - and - the left at Camden Lock," recited Jumper without taking a breath.

"Well said, Jumper, well said. Now would that line be clear, Jumper?"

Jumper said nothing.

"IS THAT LINE CLEAR?" roared Bloggs, grabbing Jumper by his kerchief and half-strangling him. Jumper staggered back, choking, and his eyes glittered with fury.

"Listen Bloggs," he said, loosening his kerchief and

coughing. "I be Jumper, and I be known right through the North London system, and not just for me jumping, Bloggs, of which you 'ave 'ad a taste, but for me track-mucking too. They all know me—now, while you've been sitting nice and comfy in your blankety station, Jumper's been up your lines day after day, yes and nights too often, mucking 'em up. Not just banging 'em about in a common-vulgar way so as when we win the war there's nought but a rotten, broken old railway for us to take over, but mucking 'em careful-like; almost affection-like I might say, but effective-like as well. Ho, yes—*very* effective-like.

"Now I puts it to you Bloggs, is it likely I'm going to tell you where them tracks be mucked? *Tell* you, and see all me cunning gone for nought? Just ain't reasonable, is it Bloggs?"

Bloggs' expression had been getting blacker and blacker while Jumper spoke, and now he leaned forward and punctuated what he had to say by jabbing his forefinger into Jumper's chest.

"Right, Jumper-me-lad, I've got the measure of *you*, and now I'll tell you what's going to 'appen to you.

"You're staying in this cab with me and Bodger and I'm going to drive full steam ahead. In case you don't know, Jumper, that means fast. Now if you think one of your booby-traps of a cunningness is coming up and you say nothing, Jumper, you and me and Bodger'll be the first to catch it. Think about that, Jumper.

"Ever been in the cab when it's going fast and it hits an hobstruction, Jumper? No, don't s'pose you 'ave. Well, I'll tell you what 'appens, Jumper; you gets boiled alive with steam and boiling water, that's what 'appens. Now Bodger and me'll take our chance and jump clear, but not you, Jumper. You'll be tied up good and proper and no-one ain't going to *un*tie you, no matter how much you jump about.

"It won't be nice, Jumper, if we *should* 'it one of your

little surprises—leastways not nice for you. So my advice is that you remember where you put 'em and shout out loud and clear and in good time. You're going to *guide* me Jumper; and now I'll tell you where I'm going first—I'm going fast down the direct line to Whittington. Tie him up nice and tight, Bodger."

He pulled the whistle.

Jumper rolled his eyes round the cab in hopeless thought.

"Better take the Reservoir loop, Bloggs," he said urgently.

Bloggs looked at him approvingly.

"*That's* better, Jumper, Keep that up all the way and we'll 'ave a nice, safe, uneventful journey."

Widgie heard the whistle and he jumped up from his tea at once.

He felt left out and ignored—having fought hard in the battle, and above all, having captured the Jumper, he felt that at least *some* reward was due to him, so he marched straight up to the engine and called out to Bloggs.

"If we're going now Mr Bloggs, I'd like to be up front in the cab with you, please."

Bloggs looked down at him, more civil than before.

"No room, young Widgie, 'cos of Jumper here and Bodger."

"Well if I can't be in the cab I'd like to be in the truck behind and on my OWN."

"In the truck behind, I don't mind, but with a guard I insist. Come 'ere, Grattle."

"Up I come, Bloggs; Grattle's always ready," and a most odd-looking Railwayman trotted up and stood at a limp attention.

Why *does* he look so odd? thought Widgie. Because his hat's crooked and his trousers are too short? No, because he's squinting and I don't know which eye to look at.

"Take this Widgie-person into the first truck, Grattle, and treat 'im kind but firm if you takes me meaning."

"I took it," said Grattle, and with a kind but firm hand

he took Widgie's arm and led him back to the first truck.

Bloggs watched them go.

"He's an asset, that boy," he said to himself. "A blooming nuisance, but an asset."

He opened the regulator and the engine chuffed heavily and began to lumber forwards, rumbling over the bridge and into the tunnel beyond.

"Coming, Jen," muttered the Asset to himself as the first truck crossed, "Won't be long now."

6

The Fleet

What *am* I doing, thought Jen, sitting in a boat in an underground canal with people called Blister and Fillbreach? Thank goodness they untied me, anyway.

"Are there any rats in the canal?" she said aloud, peering uneasily around.

Reech was lighting a storm lantern on the front of the funnel.

"'Course not—we dealt with *them* long ago." Jen shivered.

"Don't talk to the Spy," called Blister sharply, from the tiller. "She'll worm things out of you."

Jen tried to make her eyes flash indignantly all the way down the boat from her little corner in the bows but she didn't think he saw.

"Don't be silly—of course I shan't. I don't want to know anything about your rotten canals. All I want to do is to get back to the station and take Widgie home. It must be very late already and I bet we get into awful trouble when we do get back."

Blister laughed in a nasty way.

"You needn't worry about getting *back*. You're for Beasley's Arches, you are, and let the Captain see you. He's the one that makes the decisions round 'ere."

Jen held her tongue. She didn't see at the moment *how* she was going to escape, but there was no doubt in her mind that she *would*, and that probably the less she said the better.

64

She stood up so that she could see where they were going.

"Keep your head down," shouted Blister, "unless you want it knocked off—we're going into Low Tunnel any minute."

He slackened speed and steered the *Blisterlee* gently to the right, slackened off still more until they were barely moving, and then, with a quick, skilful manoeuvre, swung her hard left. Jen ducked as the fore, where she was sitting, entered a smaller canal to the left—so small that the roof was only a few inches above the funnel, and she could have reached out and touched the damp brick walls on either side.

"Stoke up, Fillbreach," shouted Blister. "I want to get through fast—I never did like Low Tunnel."

"Not yet, Blister, not yet. We'll come up to the Low Tunnel courier any minute, and ye'll need to get warnings sent on ahead."

"There he is," bellowed Reech, "I can see him to the left—slacken off, Blister."

Blister slackened speed to almost nothing and Jen saw a lantern bobbing up and down on the left hand side of the canal.

What on earth is that, she thought. There's no room for another boat in this tiny space; and then she saw the mouth of an even smaller canal with a rowing-boat in it. In the bows stood a Canaller waving a lantern.

"Who is it?" shouted Blister.

"Drinker, the courier. Who passes?"

"Blister, with a Spy. I need messages sent to Beasley's. They're coming out with a full load back at Long Shaft. We'll need to flood the Fleet and get every man out."

Drinker grinned knowingly, and tapped the side of his nose with his forefinger.

"That's not news. I was up at Long Shaft meself not quarter hour ago."

"What happened—who wins?" Blister's voice was urgent

and anxious.

"Not my job to know. I don't hang about. My job's to get news down, get it down fast and not waste time. I've already flashed them to flood Fleet—what else should I do?"

"Tell the Captain I'm on my way and that I have a Spy for him—one from up above."

"An Abovegrounder?" Drinker gave a low whistle and held his lantern up higher. "That'll please him I don't doubt, just when the Long Shafters decide to try a break-out. Alright, he'll have it long before you've even reached Angel Basin."

"I don't have time for Angel, Drinker. Straight through the Fleet for us."

"What if Fleet be flooded?"

"She'll only be in half-flood at most when we hit her, and even half-flood'll get us to Beasley's quicker than the engines would."

"Well, it's your risk Blister, your risk, but I don't want to flash the Captain and then you go and drown your Spy on the way. That's blame I can do without. I figure Fleet begins to flood in five minutes—don't forget we've got the new sluice at Shipley's now."

"My risk, Drinker, as you said. You do your job and I'll do mine."

"You're a foolhardy man, Blister. You always was and so was your father and look what happened to him. Get on your way, but watch out for the Cut. Last time Fleet flooded that's where the overflow went."

Blister gave him a look and put the throttle to 'Full Ahead.'

The *Blisterlee* swung out into the centre of Low Tunnel; the wash curved strongly backwards and black smoke belched out of the funnel as Fillbreech shovelled more coal into the fire-box.

Blister looked back and saw Drinker's lantern disappearing.

"Rather him than me—I hate them communication canals.

Low Tunnel's bad enough—them others give me the willies."

He peered ahead over the top of the cabin roof.

"We should be widening out soon, thank gawd. A man can't breathe here."

Jen turned round and leant her elbows on the forepeak so that she could see ahead—she could just have stood up but she felt uneasy with her head so close to the roof. Reech had lit two more lanterns now, and it was light enough for her to see all the little communication tunnels quite clearly. How complicated it all is, she thought. It must have taken ages to build.

The tunnel began getting higher and wider, so she stood up cautiously and looked back at the cabin and the funnel and at Blister's pointed nose poking out above them. His eyes flickered no longer but stared intently ahead, and Jen could see his hand on the high tiller, constantly shifting it a little this way and that way to adjust the course. All she could see of Fillbreach was his bottom as he kept taking shovel after shovel of coal down to the fire-box, but Reech was in full view, leaning against the front of the cabin and staring at her. "No tricks now," he said nastily, "or I'll tie you up like a trussed chicken again. You just behave yeself."

Jen turned her back on him with a gesture that she hoped was more eloquent than words, and concentrated all her attention on where they were going. Only just in time, too, because she saw that they were coming up to a sort of crossroads, and she didn't want to miss anything. In fact, she saw that it was one more than a crossroads—or whatever you call them when they're canals, she thought—because on the other side of the cross Low Tunnel split into two.

I wonder which we'll take—I hope it's the big one on the right.

The *Blisterlee* rocked a little as the cross-currents hit her, and then did indeed take the right fork, swinging smoothly into what seemed to be an unfinished canal. At any rate, the walls and roof were all of rough-hewn rock with no brick facing, and Jen was just in time to see 'New Junction Canal' painted roughly on the side as they entered it.

If only I wasn't a prisoner and Widgie-less I could quite enjoy this, thought Jen, peering into each side-tunnel as they passed it and looking up the ventilation shafts of which there seemed to be quite a number.

She wanted to ask Reech lots of questions about it all, but he was so surly and aggressive that she didn't dare. Instead, she began making a map in her head of the route they had taken, and then adding in all the side-tunnels and looping them together into a huge, imaginary network.

I suppose they've all got names like this one, she thought. What a pity they're not painted on the sides like street signs.

She heard a shout from Reech but she didn't deign to turn round this time.

"Slacken off, Blister—we're coming up to the Cut."

Are we, thought Jen. Well, I can't see it.

But then they rounded a wide, shallow bend and she did —the tunnel was dividing into two again, or rather the New Junction Canal continued on to the right and an equally wide but considerably lower tunnel bore off to the left. To her disappointment she saw the *Blisterlee* swing towards it, and although it was still much higher than Low Tunnel had been, she felt hemmed in and uncomfortable again. The ventilation shafts seemed to have stopped and it was faced with smoke-blackened bricks against which the *Blisterlee's* yellow lamps threw huge shadows.

"Not long till the Fleet now," she heard Fillbreach say. "That's when we'll have to hang on."

Jen looked round, startled—she'd forgotten about the flood—and she saw Blister's eyes flickering in the lamplight.

"We'll be alright—I ain't steered *Blisterlee* twenty year for nothing, Fillbreach."

Jen turned back and caught a glimpse of a communication canal on the left that looked so tiny that even a rowing-boat would have found difficulty in getting into it. Reech pointed to it.

"Look—water level's higher than it oughter be," he shouted.

"That's 'cos of the overflow from the Fleet like Drinker said. It comes through the communication canals—it'll help us along but there'll be a bit of undertow. Stoke up Fillbreach—we'll need more power."

Jen glanced upwards and saw that the roof looked lower than it had been. Some of the smoke from the funnel was finding its way for'ard and making her cough, so she rooted around until she found her old gag, and held it over her nose and mouth.

"Water's rising, I think," shouted Reech looking hard ahead.

Blister looked up at the roof.

"You mean the level's high—she ain't rising."

"Hard to say—I think she's rising."

"We'll be alright—there's a good two feet from roof to funnel-top."

The *Blisterlee* was riding a bit rough now, and every time they passed a communication canal Jen noticed quite a high tide of water coming out of it.

"There's not two feet now," said Reech suddenly.

Blister looked up anxiously.

"Stoke her up, Fillbreach, we'd better get through fast."

"Can't give you no more, Blister. Firebox is up to there."

"What's she doing Reech?"

"Rising for sure."

"Alright, Reech, so she's rising. But how fast?"

"Too fast, Blister. I don't like it."

"Oh, Gawd," said Blister, half to himself.

He's looking panicky, thought Jen, turning round to look at the funnel.

Fillbreach had stopped stoking and was examining the distance to the roof critically. "She's closing in, Blister. I give it not much more than a foot."

Blister looked up and saw the roof flashing by above him, and once he looked he found he couldn't stop looking. His hand on the tiller trembled and *Blisterlee's* bows began wandering.

"Keep 'er steady, Blister," said Fillbreach warningly.

Blister blinked hard, shook his head and dragged his eyes away from the roof. His hand tightened on the tiller and the *Blisterlee* straightened up.

"I'm alright, Fillbreach. You keep the fire stoked. Reech, keep your eye on that funnel-top and read me the distances."

"We're holding at a foot, Blister."

Jen looked up. The nearer the roof they got the faster it seemed to flash by and the more threatening it looked. She turned back to the others to try to see from their expressions how worried she ought to be, and she saw Blister staring up at the roof again in that odd, hypnotised way.

"You're wandering again, Blister," shouted Fillbreach. "The bows are wandering."

Something like a small tidal wave lifted the stern and the *Blisterlee* rode noticeably higher.

"Nine inches and still rising." Reech was watching the top of the funnel like a hawk.

"Hold her *steady*, Blister."

But Blister seemed to hear nothing—he was staring at the roof with vacant eyes and his tiller hand was trembling.

Reech's voice took on a new urgency.

"Rising faster, now, Only six inches left. SIX INCHES," he shouted, in case they hadn't heard him.

Fillbreach looked back anxiously at Blister, then up at the funnel, then back at Blister. He shrugged his shoulders in sudden decision and took command.

"Right, that's enough. We'll have to down funnel.

Close the throttle, Blister. BLISTER—the throttle!"

In a dream, and without taking his eyes off the roof, Blister groped for the throttle. Fillbreach grabbed the funnel-chain and threw it at Reech.

"Hold it tight while I knock the catches up, and mind you let her down gentle."

Reech held hard onto the chain while Fillbreach knocked up the two big catches. The funnel lurched forward from its base and Reech leant back on the chain and let her down to the deck as gently as he could. The firebox sent out a spray of hot sparks, and smoke billowed out in all directions. The *Blisterlee* was enveloped in thick, stinking fog.

"Damp the fire," coughed Reech, "or we'll burn above and sink below."

Fillbreach groped his way to the cabin and came up with a bucket. He leant over the gunwale, thrust it in the canal and hurled the water at the firebox. There was a great hissing and the smoke turned black and gradually cleared. With no power now, the *Blisterlee* was drifting from side to side and scraping dangerously against the canal walls.

"Get back to the platform, Reech, and grab the tiller. Blister's useless." Reech bent almost double and staggered aft where Blister was crouching on the platform with his hands on top of his head, moaning to himself. Reech seized the tiller, got her bows for'ard and let the flood-tide do the rest. Fillbreach checked that the fire was properly doused and ran back to join him. He looked at Blister.

"Is he hurt?"

"No, it's something else—I don't know what."

The *Blisterlee*'s bows were still wandering.

"Can't you hold her on course, Reech? She'll hull herself this way."

"Doing me best," grunted Reech, trying to anticipate which way the swirling currents would push her next.

Jen looked fearfully up at the roof and crouched low in the bows—she wanted to crawl back and join the others on the platform behind the cabin but she felt too frightened to move.

"She's still rising." She heard Reech's voice, panic-stricken. "What shall we do?"

"Keep yer head down and say your prayers. Can't do no more."

There was a sudden snap and Reech snatched his fingers away just in time. The top of the tiller had splintered. Reech crouched lower and tried to maintain a hold on it half-way down.

Then the grating noise started—at first intermittently as the waves thrust the roof of the cabin against the roof of the tunnel and then lowered it away again, but after a little while almost continual. They could almost measure the rate at which the water was rising by it. Finally, there was the sickening sound of wood splintering and they had to watch the whole cabin and engine-room being slowly crunched up. The red and yellow roses and castles crumbled one by one and the splintered planks were torn loose and thrust forwards into the boat.

Fillbreach and Reech were crouched low on the platform with their hands over their heads like Blister, and up in the bows Jen lay flat and held her hands over her ears so that she couldn't hear the awful noise. She tried to look up and around. The roof was almost on top of her and she could see each blackened brick as it swept by. The firebox was still smoking in the shattered engine-room and farther back she could just see three pathetic-looking bunks in the cabin.

"Oh Widgie—where *are* you?" she said out loud, thinking, I won't even be able to say goodbye.

Finally, came the noise she had been waiting for and hoping against hope would never begin. It was the roof scraping the bows and the gunwales.

I must get out *now* and swim before it's too late.

She lay flat and tried to rip the planks up from the bottom of the boat.

But what's the point if there's no space to swim *in*?

Part of the fore-end guard caught, was ripped off and fell back on her. She eased herself backwards as water began splashing in through the gap and she realized that the *Blisterlee* was making hardly any headway now that the roof was on the gunwales. The flood forced her forwards but the roof crushed her back and the poor *Blisterlee* creaked and groaned in every joint between them. Then it gave an almighty shriek and Jen saw the top of the fore-peak break inwards. She put her hands over her head and waited with her eyes tight shut. She felt quite calm, and resigned to death, but she didn't want to see anything.

Suddenly she felt the *Blisterlee* lifted high in the air and she heard a great roaring noise. It went on and on and Jen knew it must be water. The *Blisterlee* was lifted even higher but the splintering had stopped. Jen felt water rushing all over her, and then the *Blisterlee* turned right round in a full circle, twice.

"It can't—there isn't room," she said, and opened her eyes.

High above her she could just see the roof of a huge cavern.

"Get up Blister," she heard Reech shouting. "Bail for your life—we're in the Fleet."

Jen staggered to her feet and looked around wildly. She couldn't believe that the roof of the Cut was not still there, crushing them to death, yet here they were in a vast cavern as wide as two roads with an absolute torrent of water rushing through it and tossing the wreck of the *Blisterlee* in all directions at once.

She crawled back towards the wrecked cabin and found an old saucepan. She grabbed it before it was washed away, and began bailing. Reech had found the bailer and was emptying out water like a madman, and Fillbreach was at what was left of the tiller trying to keep the *Blisterlee* fore-end on. Meanwhile she wallowed helplessly, turning this way and that and shipping water all the time.

And the more water she shipped, the lower she stood and the more ponderous were her manoeuvres.

"Don't empty her," shouted Fillbreach. "The ballast steadies her."

"She'll sink if we don't."

"Maybe not." They could only just hear each other above the roaring torrent.

There was a movement on the platform, and very slowly Blister got up. He shook his head and rubbed his face with his hands—he looked as if he had just woken up—and stared around him in a puzzled way. He frowned heavily when he saw the crushed cabin and the splintered sides of the *Blisterlee*, and he gave a big sigh. Then he looked behind him and saw the raging Fleet and a new look came into his eyes.

"Right men; get that funnel up"—he sounded like a Captain again.

Fillbreach stared in disbelief.

"You'll get no fire going with a wet firebox."

"Do as I say, Fillbreach," said Blister sharply. "Leave that tiller to me."

Fillbreach hesitated, shrugged his shoulders, and started pulling on the funnel chain.

"You fix the clamps, Reech," he shouted.

Reech stopped bailing for a moment and banged down the heavy hooks.

"It's busted near the hinge, Blister."

"Never mind that—it'll do its job."

Blister looked around him.

"Now I don't care how you do it, Master Stoker Fillbreach, but get that fire lit."

"You're mad, Blister."

"GET IT LIT."

There was only one way Fillbreach could think of. With a poisonous look at Blister, he lurched aft to the windlass-hole and dragged out a can of kerosene. He threw the kerosene into the fire-box and then found an old rag and soaked it in it. Standing with his legs apart to keep his balance he began striking his tinderbox and at last he managed to get a spark onto the rag. It flared up fast—"Take cover!" he roared—and he hurled it into the firebox.

There was a great wind and the *Blisterlee* blew up.

Flames leapt fifty feet in the air and scorched the roof above, Jen fell over backwards and her eyebrows never recovered, Fillbreach was blasted straight back onto Reech and Blister fell back onto the broken tiller, but the fire was lit.

Blister jumped to his feet and rushed at the one thing he really understood—his controls.

"Dry off that engine, Reech. Fillbreach—free the rudder; she's fouled."

He checked the water-guage to see if there was still water in the boiler, and he saw a little pressure on the steam-gauge. He opened up the throttle and turned the gear-lever to forward. Nothing happened.

"Reech—raise me more steam. Throw anything you can find in that firebox."

"Come on, *Blisterlee*," he whispered. "Don't let me down, *Blisterlee*—it's not the last voyage we'll make together and that's a promise." A cloud of sparks came from the firebox as Reech fed it and he saw the steam-gauge rise a little as the pressure built up.

"Good old *Blisterlee*," he shouted suddenly, as he opened up the throttle again and felt her throbbing a little. 'She's living again,' he thought. Fillbreach hauled himself back from the stern gunwale with a length of tattered rope in his hands. He held it up for inspection.

"Rudder's free, Blister."

Blister grinned, turned the gear-lever to forward and

grabbed the remains of the tiller. The *Blisterlee* began to get herself properly fore-end on, and although the flood-tide was still pushing her faster than the engine was, Blister felt the boat respond.

"Bail out what she ships. Keep her lying low," he shouted for'ards.

There was only Jen and Fillbreach to bail because Reech was stoking the firebox with wet planks, and it was as much as they could do even to bail out what she shipped. Jen felt that the whole world was made of water—water spilling over the sides of the *Blisterlee*, water being bailed, water hurling itself and the *Blisterlee* forwards, water released and confined, water stronger than anything except the rocky walls.

Something made both Jen and Reech look up and for-wards together.

"Look out, Blister—the bend's coming up," shouted Reech.

Blister had seen it.

It was fairly sharp and Blister had negotiated it hundreds of times in the past, but not in these conditions. Now, for the first time he felt unsure of it—for one thing it looked different and for another he had never taken it this fast and in such a wreckage of a boat.

He straddled his legs wide to get a good purchase and he grasped the broken tiller with both hands. He watched carefully as the bend approached and delayed just a little longer than usual. Then he leaned hard over and hoped that the tiller and rudder would take the strain. The *Blisterlee* swung wide to the left and the bows swept round majestically. There was a crash as the back platform hit the rocky walls— Blister had misjudged it—and water began pouring into the stern.

Blister was thrown off his feet.

"Bail here, Reech. Fillbreach—here," he shouted urgently. They all rushed aft—Jen as well—while Blister regained his

feet and the tiller, and the *Blisterlee* swept round the bend
in a huge and ungoverned circle. They bailed hard to hold
their own against the rushing waters and Fillbreach did a
rough repair of the back platform with broken cabin planks
—then they all looked up to see the new stretch of water.

For a moment no-one moved or spoke.

Ahead of them was the Fleet Bridge, the graceful curves
of its huge cast-iron sides standing some fifteen feet above
the flood, but it was completely awash.

"We can't get under it," said Blister, blankly, and although
no-one could hear him they all knew what he'd said.

Finally it was Reech who pulled himself together.

"Reverse, Blister—throw her into reverse."

Blister came out of his trance, slackened off the throttle
and turned the gear-lever to backwards and the *Blisterlee*
shuddered from fore to aft as her engines tried to fight the
flood. For a wonderful moment she held her own, but
then she was seized and swept forwards again.

About half-a-mile to go, thought Blister, and the knowledge that there was nothing else he could do was like a
stone in his stomach.

He waited a moment before he gave the command and
then shouted, loud and harsh.

"Abandon ship. Jump for your lives."

No-one moved.

"JUMP," screamed Blister.

Still no-one moved, and then they suddenly heard a new
and unfamiliar sound. It wasn't the water or the boat or
Blister shouting. It seemed to come from the bridge, or
rather from the tunnel that led to the bridge. They all
stared at each other, uncomprehending.

Chuff.

Chuff, chuff, chuff.

It was Blister alone who realized what was happening.

"They'll hit flood when we hit bridge." He stared ahead
as if he was fascinated by the noise.

At first it was only the engine they saw, with Bloggs peering ahead, his hands on the controls. Then came the big tender, and Bodger was standing on top of it, on the coals, shovelling them down into the cab. Then came the first truck—

"Widgie," screamed Jen.

7

Grue's Pit

"They've beat us."

Bloggs' cry of rage and despair spurred him forwards and he began to drive the *Blogger* hell-for-leather across the flooded bridge.

"Don't do it, Bloggs"—Bodger's warning shout brought him to his senses and he realized it wouldn't work. He put the blower on, shut the regulator and braked hard. He felt the wheels lock, but they were deep in rushing water now and the engine was rocking from side to side and skidding forwards at the same time.

Bloggs had never been in a locomotive that was out of control before and the sense of its dead weight frightened him. What should he do? Open up and follow his first reaction to drive across? No—do nothing—it was beginning to lose momentum. Bloggs could hear the skid-noise deepening as it slowed down, but when it finally came to rest nearly half-way across he didn't believe it, because the whine of metal against metal continued.

He looked down, startled, to see if the *Blogger* was disintegrating beneath his feet, and there was a sharp metallic crack. One of the stanchions of the bridge, near centre, snapped, whipped upwards and stayed there like a warning finger. There was an odd grinding noise punctuated by more metallic cracks from breaking stanchions and then the two centre piers began to subside. The noise changed to a brittle roar as if a giant was crumbling up a mountain-range of brown paper and, quite suddenly, the bridge literally broke in two between the supports. The graceful sides thrust jagged arms upwards, the abutments and track collapsed inwards and the centre piers sunk with a final *plié* to the bed of the river.

Over them all surged the triumphant waters in a great wave, and in their arms they bore their prize, the wreck of the *Blisterlee*. No-one marked its passing nor heard, above the din of destruction, Blister's hysterical cry "We're through"—it was whipped on to its separate destiny while the Railwaymen faced their own.

The track was crumbling away from them and the truncated bridge was beginning to sway from side to side.

"Get her in reverse, Bloggs," shouted Bodger, watching the track from the tender.

"I daren't, Bodger—I daren't move her."

"Do it slow, Bloggs, it's your only chance."

Bloggs leant out of the cab and tried to assess how long the track would last. It seemed to be subsiding less violently now, but yet quite steadily as bolt after bolt strained and finally snapped. Bodger was right—the bridge was growing weaker every minute. With his heart in his mouth he took the brake off, put the engine in backward gear and opened the Regulator. The wheels turned but they wouldn't grip; the engine started rocking again and Bloggs could feel the supports underneath him swaying with it.

"Give her more power, Bloggs," shouted Bodger.

Bloggs knew that would be useless and he was afraid of increasing the sway—already it seemed to be widening.

"Bodger—how much of the train is on the bridge?"

Bodger peered backwards.

"Guard's Van and half of the Passenger Coach is on solid ground."

"Right—evacuate them first, and then get the rest of the men to back down the train. Tell 'em to move fast but gentle."

"There's no *time*, Bloggs—look at that track."

"TELL 'EM BODGER," roared Bloggs in a sudden fury.

He couldn't hear what Bodger shouted backwards, but he could see him gesticulating, and when he leant out of the cab he saw the Railwaymen climbing awkwardly backwards from truck to truck, while the Passenger Coach was already nearly empty.

"Tell 'em to move faster, Bodger," he shouted urgently, watching the track.

One of the wheels gripped for a moment and then spun again.

'I wonder,' thought Bloggs looking at the water.

He opened the cylinder waste cocks and the waste steam hissed out and hit the surging waters. He moved the Reversing Lever towards the centre and felt the engine move back about a foot. The wheels were still spinning but there was a little grip in them now. A wave of optimism swept over him—perhaps with a lightened load and more steam to check the waters. . .

He looked back anxiously. The front half of the train was evacuated but there was a pile-up at the back because of the difficulty of climbing from the last truck into the Passenger Coach.

How were things forward? Ten feet of solid track left and the swaying getting worse. No time to lose—it had better be now or never. Warn the men to hang on tight and then do it.

He threw his head back and roared at the top of his voice.

"Hold tight men. Hold tight—we're going to MOVE. COME ON BLOGGER," and he opened the Regulator a bit more.

The wheels screamed on the track, the steam still hissed down and checked the water, but still the *Flying Blogger* didn't move. The track crumbled faster as the engine-power jolted it and the bridge and engine rocked drunkenly together.

"Can't do more," muttered Bloggs in despair. "Let's go down in glory, anyway," and he pulled the whistle in a final, valedictory shriek.

To the end of his days Bloggs maintained it was the whistle that did it. From that moment on, the driving-wheels decided to grip, the train gave an enormous shudder from engine to guard's van and it began to lumber backwards. Bloggs gave a shout of triumph, and while he clung onto the whistle with one hand he opened the blower with the other so as not to let the wheels develop a pattern.

He looked back and saw the trucks disappearing one by one into the tunnel and the men clinging on for dear life.

"Steady Bloggs," shouted Bodger. "It's too fast."

Bloggs silently agreed, but with the sway of the bridge getting worse each second and with only twenty feet left to solid ground, he felt reckless. Holding on even harder to his talisman, the whistle, he accelerated. The *Flying Blogger* made its final lurch towards safety and the last section of the bridge gave a last agonized roar and dipped profoundly into the flood.

With a sigh, Bloggs shut the regulator, put the Reversing Lever to drifting and took his hand off the whistle. For all the noise of the rushing waters, there seemed to be a sudden hush. Then there was a muted cheer from some of the Railwaymen as they helped Bloggs down from the cab —"Bravo Bloggs," "You've done it, Bloggs," "Well done, Bloggs"—but the rest were staring down at the bridge, which lay in the flood like a twisted monument to all their endeavours.

Bloggs wiped the sweat off his face and joined them.

"That were a good bridge," said Bloggs. "My Dad helped build it."

"Ay" said Bodger.

"Solid as a rock it were, I don't care what anyone says."

"Ay."

"Them Canal Folk," said Bloggs fiercely. "I'll make 'em

pay for that bridge."

"Ay."

Bloggs turned suddenly to Jumper. "*Your* folk. It's *your* folk what done it."

Jumper went white—Bloggs looked as if he would throw him into the Fleet as well.

"I got you here safe, Bloggs," said Jumper urgently. "I got you through the Reservoir Loop *and* Great North Road *and* Spaniards with no harm come to you. Just like I said, I kept me word. Jumper's word is his bond—you know that, Bloggs."

"Ay, and I know who mucked up tracks in first place, and if they hadn't been mucked we could have gone direct via Gospel Oak and maybe got through."

"Leave 'im be, Bloggs," said Bodger wearily. "Anyway, we'll need 'im to guide us back right. We can't make Beasley's now."

There was silence in the tunnel as the full meaning of their defeat came home to them—the journey back, the mocking laughter at Long Shaft, the weary resumption of their day-to-day station life.

Bloggs looked at Jumper, then at Bodger and then at his boots.

"I ain't giving up that easy, Bodger," he said stubbornly.

"Facts is facts, Bloggs," and Bodger pointed to the remains of the bridge.

"Let's find some other facts, then. Wot about before bridge were built? How did we get to Beasley's then, eh Bodger?"

"That be afore I were born, and afore you were, Bloggs."

"Ay, but it weren't afore old Dingle were born. Where is 'e? Where's old Dingle? DINGLE!" he roared down the train. "Come up 'ere to the cab."

A bent and wizened old Railwayman shuffled up front from the back of the tunnel, looking preoccupied and at the same time mildly surprised that anyone should know he was still alive.

Widgie watched him with interest as the men made room for him to get through. "He's our oldest," whispered Grattle.

"Ay?" said Dingle, looking up at Bloggs. "Who wants Dingle?"

"Me, Dingle—I wants you. We needs your help, Dingle. Now just try and think—how did we get to Beasley's before bridge were built, Dingle?"

Dingle took off his shovel hat and scratched his bald head. Then he put it back and looked up at the roof of the tunnel and then down into the Fleet and then at Bloggs' waistcoat buttons.

"Down Grue's Pit, of course," he said.

"There y'are," said Bloggs looking round triumphantly. He turned back to Dingle. "Then why was bridge built, Dingle? There must 'ave been a reason."

"Because Grue's Pit got blocked up, Bloggs—that's why."

Bloggs looked at Bodger as if to say "I told you so."

"Then we'll *un*block it, Dingle. *That's* how we'll get through."

Dingle looked round furtively at the others, and then plucked at Bloggs' sleeve, at the same time jerking his head meaningly up at the engine cab. He climbed up inside it and Bloggs, frowning in a puzzled way, hauled himself up after him.

"I wouldn't unblock Grue's Pit if I was you, Bloggs," whispered Dingle hoarsely.

"Ho?" said Bloggs staring at him.

Dingle plucked Bloggs' sleeve again and lowered his voice still further.

"There was a reason Grue's Pit was blocked, Bloggs."

"Ho? What d'ye mean, Dingle. What reason?"

Dingle pulled at Bloggs' kerchief until his ear was nearer to him.

"The Rats," whispered Dingle. "They were big 'uns.

Maneaters."

Bloggs straightened up and looked all around him at the silent ranks of Railwaymen.

"Right, men—everyone back to the trucks. We'll be moving in five minutes. Bodger—you wait down there with Jumper. Grattle—take the Widgie-boy back to the first truck. See 'em all in, Mr Guard, and make sure we get the order right."

He turned back to Dingle.

"Tell me quick, Dingle," he whispered. "Tell me what 'appened."

Dingle gave him a heavy, conspiratorial wink and waited until the men were out of earshot.

"It were a right *war*, Bloggs. I were only a young 'un but I remembers it. We all figured it were the Canallers' fault for not keeping 'em down, because that's where they bred—allus by the Canals—but in the end we had to do something or them Rats were like to take over the whole system. So we fought 'em, best ways we could, and them Canallers never so much as lent an 'and. Fact, 'twas worse than that—while we was fighting Rats them Canallers took advantage and captured Beasley's again." Bloggs frowned.

"So what do we do, Bloggs? We fight 'em and we entice 'em—part and part—into Grue's Pit, and then we blocks up our end. We figured they'd get out far end at Beasley's and eat up them Canallers, but they never did. We never knew why. They were man-eaters too, like I said."

Bloggs eyes glittered.

"Then we'll find out why, won't we Dingle? Now's ye chance to find out."

Dingle gave a big sigh and shook his head.

"No, Bloggs. I be too old for Rats. You young 'uns do what you like but I'm going home."

Bloggs looked at him sharply.

"But I ain't *asking* you Dingle; I ain't asking you nothing. I'm *telling* you. I need you to get us there, Dingle. What 'appens when we get there is another matter and I don't have no wish to make a man do what 'e don't want; but I *orders* you to get us there. I think you'll agree that that's all fair and aboveboard and according to the Rules."

Dingle looked thoughtfully at Bloggs for a long while and then he gave an even bigger sigh. "You're a hard man, Bloggs," he said.

"That's better," said Bloggs approvingly, clapping him on the back.

"Hey, Bodger—bring that Jumper up in the cab with you. Old Dingle here's going to get us to Grue's Pit."

He opened the regulator and began reversing again, while Bodger started stoking the furnace.

"Directions, Dingle, directions," shouted Bloggs, in high good humour, "I'll go slow so's you don't get muddled."

"Go back towards Gospel Oak," said Dingle in a sad and resigned voice.

The train began lumbering backwards the way it had come, and after about ten minutes they came within sight of the East Heath turn-off. Bloggs slowed down.

"Now, wait a minute, all," he said, shutting off steam and applying the brakes. He looked at Jumper. "You brought us via Spaniards and East Heath, and Dingle wants us to go back past Savernake to Gospel Oak. How are the tracks that way, Jumper? Mucked?" Jumper nodded guiltily.

"Not as far as Gospel Oak, Dingle doesn't want you to go," said Dingle quickly. "Only as far as Savernake Siding."

Bloggs looked at Jumper enquiringly, while Jumper hopped from one leg to another in an agitation of thought.

"That be clear as long as you don't go no nearer Gospel Oak than you can 'elp," he said at last, and added sadly, "Most of me mucks seem to 'ave been made good, anyway."

"Right, Jumper," said Bloggs grimly. "I hope you're right. Bodger—get down and switch over the points."

Bodger did as he was bid and climbed back into the cab,

and the *Flying Blogger* reversed into the fork towards Savernake Road. As they approached the station Bodger said, "Tell 'em, Bloggs. Tell 'em what we're doing. Put out an Emergency Call and we'll have the whole network behind us."

Bloggs frowned. "I told you on the way down—I'll tell you again, Bodger. This is the Long Shafters' battle. *We've* got the Widgie-boy, *we'll* win the battle and *we'll* get the glory. 'Sides, I 'aven't noticed them putting too much effort into helping us these last three years we've been blocked up. Not too much. Ho, no."

He waved in a lordly way as they passed the station, and the Savernake Railwaymen stared open-mouthed at seeing a Long Shaft engine on the tracks again. Once past the station, Bloggs cast a satisfied eye at Bodger, slowed down, and began creeping at snail's pace.

"Watch out behind, Jumper. I wouldn't like to be in your shoes if the Guard's Van hits one of your booby-traps of a cunningness."

"Savernake Siding coming up," shouted Bodger, looking back.

"I 'opes you know what you're doing, Dingle," said Bloggs, shutting off steam. "The Siding's a dead end."

The points swung into view.

"Tell 'im to switch 'em over, Bloggs, and go forwards slow," said Dingle, getting caught up in the excitement.

Bodger gave him a look, and climbed down with dignity to switch the points again, and the engine chuffed slowly forwards into the narrow siding. Behind them came the confused muttering from the Railwaymen, growing louder as they went further in. Bloggs realized that the time had come to eke out a bit of information, and he shouted back as loud as he could.

"Alright, men. We're only going along the Old Route to Beasley's. You'll get ye chance for a fight soon enough."

"Ay, that they will," muttered Dingle, "and not the sort

they're thinking of. Alright, Bloggs," he said aloud, "stop 'er again—I'll do this one meself."

He hopped down from the cab, nimble as a cricket now that he was in charge, and began feeling the wall of the tunnel.

"Nothing but danged cobwebs," he grumbled. "Hasn't been used for years I wouldn't think."

Bloggs watched impatiently while Dingle hobbled up and down, peering at the tunnel walls. Eventually he stopped, brushed the cobwebs off the brickwork, and grunted: "Ah—knew it was 'ere somewheres." Widgie, who loved this sort of thing, leant out of his truck and watched closely. Dingle was trying to prise out a brick, and at last, by wiggling it around, he managed it. He put his hand into the open space and hauled out two more, exposing an old handle.

"They bricked it up after you-know-what," he said over his shoulder to Bloggs. He wrestled with the handle. "Can't shift it," he muttered crossly to himself. "Give me some oil, Bloggs."

Bloggs handed him down an old oil-can with a long spout, and Dingle squirted oil all over the handle and rubbed it in the joints.

"H'm, that's better—people should keep things oiled. Sheer carelessness."

He heaved the handle up, then down, then up again and finally managed to twist it full circle. There was a slow grinding noise ahead.

"Alright, Bloggs." Dingle darted back into the cab. "Slow ahead—no, no, no—*dead* slow."

Bloggs edged forwards, and fifty yards ahead he could see the dead-end bumpers looming up.

"The bumpers, Dingle," he shouted.

"You won't hit *them*," said Dingle. "Trust Dingle, Bloggs. Slower now—down to walking pace."

The engine crept forwards, and within ten feet of the bumpers it suddenly jolted to the left and began creeping down another siding like a rather small 'Tunnel of Love' at a fairground.

"Hidden points," said Dingle proudly. "Me Dad made 'em—they links us up with the Eastern Line, but they ain't been used these fifty year. You're alright now, Bloggs, if you go steady. It's rusty, but it's moderate safe."

This is a really secret railway, thought Widgie. It must be if not even Bloggs knew about it.

"Is it alright, Bloggs?" came shouts from the men farther back.

"Safe as 'ouses," shouted Bloggs, although the rustiness of the track and the narrowness of the tunnel were not at all to his liking. Also there was very little light, so that he had to rely largely on the big reflector lamps on the front of the engine—they gave a very spooky light, Widgie decided, knocking back cobwebs that all seemed to fall straight into the first truck. Grattle found a stick and began using it to push them away.

The line kept twisting and turning but always bearing to the right, and at one point there was a sudden hollow sound as the track went over a wooden bridge.

"A *wooden* bridge," said Bloggs uneasily.

"The old Fleet before it were diverted further south," said Dingle, looking over the side at the dried-up river bed.

Bodger stopped stoking and cocked an ear. "What's that? There's water ahead."

Bloggs looked questioningly at Dingle.

"That be the New Junction Canal—it goes over us further up—it's deepish, this Old Route."

The noise of the water got louder until they could hear it right over their heads. "It never used to be that loud," said Dingle, interested, and just as he said it, it started raining.

"What the devil?" said Bloggs, staring up at the roof where the water was seeping fast through the rocks. "We'll have to get that fixed, Dingle, if we keep this route open.

It's them Canallers again, mucking things up for us." He looked accusingly at Jumper.

The track turned sharply to the right and the tunnel widened ahead where three sets of tracks developed from their single line.

"Hold it, Bloggs," shouted Dingle. "Let me get them points in order—it's the Old Grafton Junction coming up." He nipped down and moved a pair of old points cautiously until he saw the tracks point to the right again. "The other two go orf to the Great East Line. Steady ahead now Bloggs, or you'll come a cropper."

Bloggs slowed to almost walking pace again, and the tunnel not only widened still more but got higher and higher until they were in a large and rather cold cavern. The three tracks had multiplied into about twenty now, and the train was continually jolting over rusty sets of points.

"Are we right, Dingle?" asked Bloggs anxiously.

"Should be, Bloggs. 'Twas only them two further back that'd take us wrong. These are just shunting tracks and sidings."

The Old Junction had plenty of ventilation shafts so that everything was clearly, if dimly, visible, and the Railwaymen observed everything with the greatest professional interest—old engine sheds, obsolete rolling stock labelled G.E.L., even two old tank locomotives.

"Proper busy, this were once," said Dingle, peering around. "See that signal-box? I used to work there with me Dad. Had to keep your eyes skinned in those days, I can tell you. Shunting trucks in and out of the sheds and down to King's Cross, and then all the big stuff going out East, and Station Masters rushing up and telling you you'd done it all wrong, and all the noise and bustle. Hardly time for a cup o' tea. Pity it's all gone and forgotten."

It took the Blogger nearly five minutes to lumber through the junction, and then there were so many different exits that Bloggs had to stop while Dingle ran from one to the other trying to decide which they should take. Eventually, for no reason apparent to anyone else, he chose one, set the points and climbed back into the cab.

"I 'ope that's the right one," said Bloggs suspiciously.

"Trust Dingle—'e'll get you there. Though later on you may wish 'e 'adn't," he added darkly.

Bloggs tried not to look irritated, and edged the *Blogger* forward into the new tunnel, which was quite large and airy with two sets of tracks and every now and then a maintenance hut let into the wall. He opened the regulator and the *Blogger* made good speed for a while, but then the tunnel began closing in again and reduced itself to a single-track for the iron bridge over New Canal. Bloggs held his breath as they went over, but there were no barges nor any Canallers in sight.

"Slower, Bloggs—it gets proper narrow soon," said Dingle, peering ahead.

"Don't see why we couldn't have used the New Junction Line for this bit," grumbled Bloggs.

"They never linked the Old Route up with it—more fool they. Anyway the New Line don't go past Caledonian now. No, Bloggs; you listen to old Dingle—this is the only way to where you're going."

There were quite a few sidings opening off the Old Route now, and Bloggs had to keep stopping while Bodger got down and wrestled with rusty points—"'e can do 'em now—they're easy ones," Dingle had said. They crossed one more iron bridge over a disused canal, and then, as the tunnel began to narrow, so the signs began.

OUT OF ORDER AT 2000 YARDS, painted in dirty white on the tunnel wall to their left.

Bloggs cocked a shrewd eye at it and decided to let the men draw their own conclusions before he spoke to them.

DEAD END—GRUE'S PIT in uneven letters on an old wooden signpost.

He slackened speed and glanced round at Dingle. The old

man was looking a bit white and trembly—I'll let him off the hook when we gets there, he thought.

DANGER AT 500 YARDS.

He slowed down to walking-pace, and rehearsed in his mind what he was going to say to the men.

GRUE'S PIT—KEEP OUT.

Finally there was a huge wooden plank suspended from the roof:

DANGER. RATS. DO NOT DESTROY BARRIER.

It was the end of the road—ten yards ahead was a rough-built wall right across the tunnel and painted across it were the words:

DO NOT TOUCH THESE ROCKS.

Bloggs stopped the engine, wiped his hands on some cotton waste, and shouted down the train as loudly as he could, "Everyone out. We 'ave a decision to decide."

The Railwaymen tumbled out from the trucks and from the Passenger Coach, still holding their picks and shovels and crowbars, and crowded up towards the engine.

"You saw them signs?" said Bloggs loudly and clearly. "Anyone a-scared of Rats?"

"NO."

"Rats is just rats."

"On to Beasley's and bash 'em."

"Right," said Bloggs, with a touch of pride in his voice. "I'm with you there. Now I propose to give you a plan of campaign. If we're to get the train through, we've got to bash this 'ere wall down. But if we bashes wall down the Rats get out, if Rats there be, and I don't want to risk it. So what do we do?"

"Bash it down just the same and whack 'em."

"No, we doesn't do that—we plays safe. We doesn't BASH it, we THINS it. Nice and slow and gentle, layer by layer, stone by stone, and when we judge it's thin enough we—"

"Bash it," came a voice.

"We gets the *Flying Blogger* to bash it," corrected Bloggs very firmly. "We all gets into the trucks and we backs down half-a-mile, so I can get a bit o' speed up, and *then* we bashes it, and then we drive full speed through the Pit and we come out at Beasley's and then—"

"We really bash 'em. 'Ooray, 'ooray."

"They'll get us just the same," muttered Dingle.

"Shut up, Dingle," said Bloggs sharply. "They may not even be there by now. Exterminated by Canal Folk as like as not, or just died off."

"They don't die off, they just breed," said Dingle mournfully.

Bloggs turned away impatiently.

"Now, work easy, men. One rock at a time and form a chain to get them out of the road, but keep the tracks clear. There's only room for ten men at the face, so take it in turns. Dingle—you stay with me and this Jumper-man in the cab. Grattle, take the Widgie-boy to truck five and stand guard over 'im 'cos I want 'im safe. I got plans for 'im."

Widgie stood up in his truck indignantly, and protested in a loud voice: "Listen Bloggs—that's not fair. Who captured Jumper? Who helped you win Long Shaft? I want to stay in the cab with you and the others where I can see everything that's going on. Anyway, you know by now I'm a good fighter, and also I'm not scared of Rats. At least, I haven't seen any yet but I bet I wouldn't be. I've got hamsters at home and they're like small rats and I can understand every word they say, and they can understand me, what's more." He stopped for lack of breath.

Bloggs stared at him.

"Alright, you can come up here for now. But if I say you go back, you go back and no argey-bargey. Understood?"

So Widgie climbed into the cab and watched as one stone after another was cautiously removed from the Barrier to Grue's Pit.

INTERLUDE II

284 Cranley Gardens,
Muswell Hill

"I don't care if we are supposed to stay by the phone," said Mrs. Widgeon; "I'm going up to the Embankment to see what's going on. I can't just keep sitting here doing nothing but think, and anyway it'll be dark soon and we shan't be able to see."

"No you don't, my dear," said Mr. Widgeon firmly. "You'd trip over and sprain your ankle or something. No, if anyone goes I do, but I've been thinking about it for the last half-hour and it really won't work. I mean if, or rather *when* the police ring up, I'll probably have to go and collect them both, and you don't drive and they may be quite a long way off, and—"

"Well, why *don't* the police ring then? I mean, it's been ages. They might think of giving us some news or something instead of just leaving us here guessing."

"I suppose they might; I hadn't thought of that. Yes, I'll ring them. Good idea—get a progress report."

So he got up and went to the telephone in the hall, and Mrs. Widgeon stood in the kitchen doorway listening and trying to guess the other end of the conversation.

"Hallo? Yes, it's Mr. Widgeon speaking . . . about two kids . . . well, my wife's naturally a bit worried, and so am I come to that, so I wondered if you could give us a bit of news; I mean tell us what's happened so far. What? Oh, you've radioed all your cars . . . yes . . . and what about up at the Embankment . . . They're searching the tunnel? They're searching the tunnel, Mum . . . And their walkie-talkies won't work in it so you don't ... What's that? Of course they're sensible kids ... No, they wouldn't go off with strange men. Well, I've told them often enough ... Yes, all our relatives are on the phone ... of course they'd ring us if ... Look, if they'd got run over you'd have a report, wouldn't you? Yes. Alright, if you say so, no news *is* good news. Thank you. Good-bye."

He went back to his wife and they both dragged themselves into the kitchen and sat down at the table again.

"Well, you heard all that. No news. That means good news according to them. Look here, old dear, can't I persuade you to take some of those sleepers the doctor gave you and go and have a lie down?"

"No, you certainly can't and I'm surprised at your suggesting it."

"Well, it was them actually. I mean, they don't want you to get in a state."

"*Get* in a state? I *am* in a state, and I can't think of anyone except an absolute vegetable who wouldn't be in a state. What does everyone expect me to do—sit down and knit? Oh darling, I'm sorry," she went on "It's just that I'm all edges. I tell you what—let's try using our brains—after all, we know our kids better than anyone else."

"Well, there's so little to use our brains *on*, but alright—good idea—let's start right back at the beginning. Now, you say they left here at about ten-thirty, give or take."

"Yes, *with* a plastic bag for their sandwiches and thermos."

"That's already unlike them—to carry a plastic bag, I mean. They hate the things, and just for a packet of sandwiches and a thermos..."

"Dad, you're right." She sat up, quite excited. "And come to think of it, it did look a bit heavy as well. And—yes, I remember now—Widgie went into the garden while I was making the sandwiches instead of standing over me watching as he usually does. I bet he went out to the garden shed and pinched that old fire-shovel or some tools or something. I say—you don't think they're digging a huge hole somewhere so that Widgie can get to Australia?"

"I wish I'd let him dig up the whole garden now."

"Don't worry about that, darling." Mrs. Widgeon patted his hand. "It hasn't happened because of your potato patch, you know."

"Well anyway, let's get back. What do we know? We know they were carrying something, probably tools and a shovel, in the plastic bag and we know that they went to the Embankment. At least, that's where they said they were going and they don't tell lies, do they? I mean, they only leave things out. Now which way would they turn when they got up there?"

"I'm sure the police were right about that—towards the old tunnel. They wouldn't be able to resist it."

"And if they'd gone straight through and out the other end?"

"I would have thought the police would have caught up with them or they'd have been so conspicuous they'd have been seen by now."

"But if they'd found an opening off the tunnel . . . that might explain why they needed the tools. In which case you were right—they *could* get lost in a tunnel."

"Oh, darling, I'm sure we're right. Ring up the police again and tell them. Tell them about the tools as well. Tell them we're sure there must be an opening *somewhere* in that tunnel."

He got up looking determined and went out into the hall again.

"Hallo, this is Mr. Widgeon speaking again . . ."

8

Beasley's Arches

Jen was so excited and bewildered at seeing Widgie again that she totally missed the drama of the *Blisterlee's* salvation.

Not so the others. They saw the big black girders looming above them, and themselves poised on the very brink of destruction, and they involuntarily put their hands over their heads and waited. It was the noise of the thousand-gun salute as the bridge snapped that made them look up, to see the wreckage flashing past them as the *Blisterlee* rode triumphantly through the gap.

Blister gave an inarticulate cry and staggered to the tiller, his attention already focused on steering them through the next bend. As for Jen, she just kept staring at the train, her mind in a turmoil of unanswered questions, until the *Blisterlee* took the bend and both the train and the bridge disappeared. Unwillingly, she was dragged back to the world of water and boats once more.

"We'll be out of the Fleet soon—" It was Fillbreach who was shouting.

"Ay, if I can get the bows into Primrose Canal."

"There she comes, Blister—coming up on the right."

Blister saw the tunnel opening about a hundred yards ahead, on the right. "Hold tight," he shouted. "I'm going in."

He threw the *Blisterlee* once more into reverse and at the same time he swung the tiller hard over. The bows turned to the right and the *Blisterlee* lurched heavily as the flood hit her broadside on.

"Watch out—you'll have her over." Reech's voice was panicky.

Blister grinned, remembering his own collapse in the Cut.

"Blister's in charge, Reech"—he suddenly opened up the throttle, and the boat recovered and began edging towards the side. Reech grabbed a boathook from under the gunwales and stood himself in the bows.

"You're overshooting her, Blister," he shouted.

Blister saw what was happening, slackened off slightly and leaned harder on the tiller, and at the crucial moment, when the bows were almost past the entrance, Reech thrust the boathook into the wall. It snapped on impact, but he thrust again with the broken end, strained against it, and brought the bows round. The aft swung in a half circle until the boat was almost fore-end on to the flood, and then Blister wrenched the tiller round in the same direction as the swing. The *Blisterlee* scraped hard against the edge of the tunnel, but she got her bows in, and while Fillbreach and Reech pushed her off the wall Blister gave the tiller a slight push to help her through. At last, he got the whole boat in and he steered her forwards for about a hundred yards before closing the throttle. They sank back, exhausted. The silence was wonderful, as the gentle waters of the canal lapped against the gunwales.

No-one spoke for a long while, and then Fillbreach got up and said, "What d'ye think happened, Blister?"

"Dunno. Maybe those new sluices at Shipley's got stuck."

"Hope we never see the Fleet like that again."

"Look at *Blisterlee*."

"Fit for the scrapyard."

"She floats."

"*And* the engine goes."

"Just goes."

"Think Bloggs and his lot went in?"

"May have done—anyway they can't make Beasley's now."

"Ay."

"We'd best make it ourselves though, and see the Cap'n. Come on—bestir yeselves."

Jen wanted to tell them about Widgie, but then she thought better of it. She didn't know if they'd seen him, or heard her shout in the excitement of the moment, and something told her not to volunteer information.

Blister opened up again and Fillbreach began feeding the firebox with wood from the broken cabin. The *Blisterlee* puttered along peacefully, just as if none of its terrible adventures had happened, and after about five minutes they came across another courier waving his lantern from a communications canal.

"Who passes?"

Blister slowed down. "The *Blisterlee* with a Spy."

The courier stared blankly.

"Well, blow me lantern down. Have you come through the Fleet?"

"Ay."

"Looks like it. We'd given you up for lost."

"So had we."

"Well, well—there's not much of *your* boat left, is there? On you go then. The Captain's waiting on ye, but not necessarily expecting ye, if you take me meaning. I'll let you take your own news."

Blister moved the gear-lever to forward, and as they drove on, the canal got higher and wider, and then divided itself into three.

Blister took the middle one, and quite soon *that* became wider and then divided itself, this time into four, and Jen realized that Beasley's Arches, when they got there, would turn out to be quite a metropolis.

They began passing other boats now, all laden with sacks of merchandise or coal, and the Canallers steering them stared open-mouthed at the *Blisterlee* as they passed. Blister ignored them all and concentrated on getting his crippled boat into the right lanes, but Fillbreach and Reech waved excitedly to friends and exchanged remarks like, "What a trip," "Lucky to get through," and "Tell you about it this evening." Once they passed a wide barge carrying about a hundred Canallers, and they all cheered and shouted "Bravo, Blister," and a glint of satisfaction appeared in Blister's eyes.

Jen had given up counting how many canals they had divided into by then and she was sitting on the gunwales enjoying the curious stares of the Canallers as they passed—they were very well-mannered, she decided, because they didn't make rude remarks or anything like that, merely looked. And then, just as she was thinking what a long way Beasley's Arches were, the canal opened up into a big basin. There were barges and narrow-boats moored along the sides, many of which appeared to be lived in, because washing hung in lines along the side of the cabins and smoke curled gently up from the funnels. An old railway bridge crossed over it from two tunnels high up in the walls, and above it was a large ventilation shaft. The basin made a left turn just after the bridge and, as Blister swung his boat round it, Jen had her first sight of Beasley's.

It was brilliant with yellow light from hundreds of lanterns which hung from the high brick walls, and there were twenty or thirty long stone jetties which were alive with bustling Canal Folk carrying goods to and from their boats. At the far end the jetties led to a wide market square bounded to left and right by long arcades of high, elegant arches. In the middle there was a statue of a Canaller with a peaked cap pointing upwards away from the jetties, where the ground rose steeply to a wide rocky hill with three sets of steps curving up it. It culminated in a high wall of rock dotted with windows and doors—like the front of high-rise blocks, thought Jen—and each door had a long wooden ladder leading up to it. The windows were all lit up and she could see people in the rooms cooking and cleaning—it all looked very cosy, she decided enviously, wishing she were back in her bedroom at home.

The arrival of the *Blisterlee* caused quite a flurry of curiosity, and the Canallers all gathered round to watch while Blister found an empty space and tied her up, but Blister himself took no notice of anyone, but just said, "Come on, Spy," to Jen and led her down the jetty.

When they got to the square he took her arm firmly, but not unkindly, and led her towards the Arches on the right. As they passed the statue, Jen saw that it said, "To the memory of Canal Folk killed in the Great Battle," but Blister wouldn't let her stop to look at anything properly. He hurried her on to the Arches and as they passed through them into the gloom of the arcades, Jen saw that each Arch led to a high corridor. It was down one of these that Blister took her. It was lit only by the occasional lantern, but in the gloom, Jen could see that heavy wooden doors were let into the walls at intervals. The corridor was very long and straight and at the end of it was another wooden door larger than the others. Blister marched straight up to it and banged hard.

"Ay?" said a voice from within, very loud and sharp.

"Blister reporting with a Spy."

"Come in, then."

Blister pushed the door open and Jen found herself in a very large stone room. It was absolutely square, and un-furnished except for a huge, roughly-made wooden table, with behind it a chair so high-backed and elaborate that it was almost a throne. Sitting in it, and totally dwarfed by it, was a man, hunched up over a large map that was spread out over the table.

He looked up as they came in and Jen saw that he had only one eye—a very shrewd and piercing eye. Over the other was a black patch and everything else he wore was black as well, from his peaked cap to his leather boots. He heaved himself up from the huge chair with difficulty, and limped round the table towards them, leaning heavily on a thick stick, which had the effect of hunching up one of his shoulders so that it looked much higher than the other.

He took no notice at all of Jen and addressed himself to Blister.

"So it's bad news, Blister. The Battle for Long Shaft lost, Bloggs and his men out in force and a Spy from Above to deal with as well."

"Not that bad, Cap'n. The Fleet Bridge is down and the Railwaymen are either in the Fleet with their train, or else cut off. Either way they can't get to Beasley's, so you've one worry less."

The Captain banged his stick on the ground.

"Better, Blister, better. Our men at Shipley's did well."

"Ay, you could call it well," said Blister, bitterly. "Wrecked the *Blisterlee* and nearly killed us."

"How so?"

"I don't know *how* so, I only know it was so. Something must've gone wrong at the new sluice. The water overflowed into the Cut and filled it up while we were in it, and the Fleet'll be impassable for days—it's boiling."

"But they couldn't have brought the Bridge down else?"

"That's as maybe. All I say is, the first time they use it this is what happens. We don't need the bridge down—it were a good bridge and one day we'll need it. Bloggs and his lot could've been stopped just as well by flooding it normal like. Since when has it been policy to break up good bridges?"

The Captain nodded to himself.

"Ay, you're right. I'll send some men up to Shipley's to find out what went wrong."

"Tell 'em to let the Shipley's men know they can pay for my repairs while they're about it. And tell 'em they'll have to take the long route. They can't get up the Fleet."

"That's clear. Now what about this Spy?" His eye flickered round to Jen. "How much of a nuisance is she going to be? Eh—Spy?"

Jen found she very much disliked being spoken of in the Third Person as if she was a bucket or something, so she answered up rather crossly.

"First of all, I'm not a Spy—I'm Jen. And second, if you don't want me to be a nuisance all you have to do is let me go and I won't trouble you any more."

The Captain gave a bitter laugh.

"Too late for that, Spy. You should've thought of that before you came down 'ere. How *did* you get down 'ere, by the bye?"

"We came through the bump in the Pit," said Jen hoping he hadn't noticed the 'we'.

The Captain looked enquiringly at Blister.

"Long Shaft Station she came from. Must be an Observation Shaft there," said Blister.

The Captain nodded to himself again and said nothing.

"What d'ye mean—'we'?" he said suddenly, looking sharply at Jen.

"My brother and me—we came together."

The Captain gave a sigh of resignation and limped back to the table.

"Not good, Blister," he said, perching himself on the edge and looking closely at his stick. "Where is the boy now?"

"I dunno. He may have been locked up at Long Shaft, or he may 'ave been with the train. If the latter, he's either at the bottom of the Fleet or wherever Bloggs is now. Our couriers ought to know. Either way, 'e won't be wandering around loose—Bloggs'll see to that. Or else the Fleet's seen to it already," said Blister grimly, as an afterthought.

Jen decided it was time for her to speak up.

"Listen, Mr Captain; if you let me go, *I'll* find Widgie, and if you let us go home after that, we'll never disturb you again or say a word to anyone about you. You have my promise, and Widgie and me are very good at not saying anything. You ask anyone—we're known for it. Besides, I'll swear on the Bible or on anything else you like. We never knew you were down here, so it stands to reason we couldn't have been *looking* for you. . ."

The Captain banged his stick on the table so hard that Jen nearly jumped out of her skin. He leant forward and put his face very near Jen's.

"Listen Spy—you leave *me* to tell *you* what I'm going to do. I ain't interested in your 'ifs' and 'buts' and 'wherefores'. I'm only interested in the simplest way of dealing with you so that you never cause mischief again.

"This 'ere world is *our* world, Spy, and there's not one of us—Canallers or Railwaymen alike—who'd let you get back above ground to blab away about us. We knows them up there—once they finds us they destroys us.

"I'll tell you something else, Spy. Once before, an Abovegrounder got down 'ere, and he was kept 'ere till he died fifty year later. It's all in the Legends, all writ up proper, and in proper detail too, but that's all you gets to know, and I only tells you so you can prepare your mind for it, 'cos I wouldn't wish you to think it's going to be a short business. As for your brother—if he's dead he's dead and good riddance, and if he's not I shall get 'im. Now be quiet."

It was as much as Jen could do to restrain herself from hitting him after those heartless words about Widgie, but she was determined not to jeopardize her chances of escape so she just clenched her hands and said nothing. Meanwhile, the Captain turned to Blister again.

"To business," he said, holding a hand out and ticking the items off on his fingers while he spoke. "First I'll get a boat up to Shipley's with a good engineer on it to look at that sluice. Next, I'll get a couple of couriers up to the bridge to see what happened to the train. Third, I'm going to teach them Railwaymen a lesson they won't forget in a hurry. I'll mobilize every man I can find and we'll hammer them out further East. It's time the North London system were ours, and them Long Shafters have given me the excuse. We'll take each station piece-meal and we'll take Long Shaft last, and then we'll transport 'em in trainloads out on the Eastern Line.

"You stand by for orders, Blister, but first take our Spy down to the deep dungeons and let her cool her heels for a bit. If she behaves 'erself we'll let her up a bit higher later on, but it won't be yet. You'd best get your boat repaired after that."

The Captain limped back to his chair, sat down at his map and said not another word.

"Ay, ay Cap'n," said Blister. "Come on, Spy," and he led Jen out of the room, slamming the door behind him.

Shall I hit him and try a run for it? thought Jen once they were in the corridor, but then she remembered all the Canal Folk on the jetties. No, better not—there'll be no escape by running in this place, only by creeping, and she let Blister lead her back the way they'd come.

They didn't go as far as the square this time though, because Blister pushed open one of the big wooden doors on their left and shoved her through. Inside there was a stone spiral staircase leading downwards.

"Straight down, Spy, and no nonsense neither," he said, pointing to it. "I've got me knife out now and it's going to be an inch away from the back of your neck."

Jen shivered—not because she was cold—and together they began descending the stone steps. They were very old, she could tell, because there were deep indentations in the middle of each one. At every bend there was a lighted lantern and as they descended deeper the steps got narrower. Jen had begun counting them when they started off, and when she had got to a hundred and sixty-two they came to a fork, with one set of spirals going to the left and another to the right. Blister pricked the point of his knife into her neck.

"Ow," said Jen indignantly.

"Left," he grunted, and they carried on down. "Hundred-sixty-three, hundred-sixty-four," said Jen wearily to herself. When she had got to two hundred and eighty-three they came to the bottom. They led into a wide stone corridor and on the right were six doors with grilles let into them. Jen was sure that one of these would be her prison, but Blister pushed her past them and into a passage to the left. There were no steps this time, but it sloped downwards quite steeply and curved this way and that as if it couldn't decide where to go.

Jen was counting paces this time and she began shivering again, but this time it was from the cold. She noticed that the walls were wet with moisture and that the lanterns were flickering

How c˙   ˙ought, there's quite a strong draught of ˙˙   ˙ up. It wasn't very nice air though, and smelt fo˙

1 wonder how deep we are—ninety-five, ninety-six—certainly deeper than *I've* ever been, and she began thinking of Widgie and Australia again, although this time in a rather different light.

She was just counting "hundred and twenty" when the passage took one more abrupt turn and she found herself facing a canal full not so much of water as green slime. "*That's* where the smell came from," she said to herself.

"Left," said Blister threateningly, as if he thought she might jump in.

There was a fairly wide towing-path beside the canal, so Jen turned obediently left along it, noticing, as she went, a rowing-boat with oars in it tied up to a bollard on the path.

That'll come in handy, she thought, although the idea of actually rowing through the green slime with the smell filled her with horror.

She began counting again—what a bore it is, she thought —but after only twenty-three paces they came to a small wooden door in the wall on their left. This one had no grille let into it.

"Inside," said Blister, and he reached past her and opened the door. Then he gave her a shove, and she half-fell in and heard the door slammed behind her, heard a key turn and heard Blister's footsteps receding the way they had come.

The dungeon was lit by the inevitable lantern on the wall, and it was almost exactly square—about twelve feet by twelve, Jen calculated. All that was in it was a small wooden bed with no mattress, but with a pillow and a blanket, and a toilet bucket.

Jen went over and examined the lantern.

When someone comes to bring me food, he'll get that in his face for a start, she decided. She took it off its hook and tried to find out how to hold it for throwing, without burning herself. Then she thought, also I must try to pick the lock, which would be a better way, because I don't really want to throw lanterns at people.

She looked everywhere for something to put in it, so that she could fiddle it around until it opened, but all she could find was the lever for the lantern's wick, and that would have meant putting it out.

In the end she just sat on the bed, with the lantern in her hand, waiting for the food-man to come.

It was only after two or three hours that it occurred to her that perhaps they weren't going to bring her any food.

9

The Ride through Grue's Pit

Widgie was not in the least worried about what was on the other side of the barrier to Grue's Pit, but he *was* excited.

It was all those signs that had played on his imagination, and also the thought that at the other end of Grue's Pit there would be another hectic fight at the end of which he would rescue Jen. So, as each rock was removed from the barrier, he felt happier and tinglier all over. He asked Bloggs if he couldn't join in with the rocks because he would be particularly good with the higher ones, but Bloggs told him sharply to stay where he was.

After they'd all been working for about half-an-hour, Dingle said, "Listen—I can hear 'em." Everyone stopped and listened and they could just hear a scrabbling noise and a thin squeaking from many voices.

"They're looking forward to getting out," thought Widgie. "I *can* understand them—I thought maybe I wouldn't be able to, but they're just like big hamsters."

Bloggs cast an experienced eye over the rocks.

"Careful now, men—we're getting near. Stone at a time and no holes."

The Railwaymen began moving with more caution, and every rock was closely examined and tested before it was taken away.

"Easy does it," said Bloggs anxiously—the scrabbling was getting louder. Then from his left came a sudden "Ow!"

"Block it up," said Bloggs sharply. "What 'appened?"

"Got bit," mumbled someone.

"Bring it 'ere," said Bloggs, "Let's have a look."

A Railwayman came over and held up his hand—it was covered with blood. Bloggs looked away and nearly shouted "Stop." Instead he said, "Alright men—they're there and they're big. Now all stop for a minute, and let's what's called consider." He hitched up his trousers and raised his voice so that those at the end of the chain could hear him.

"Can everyone 'ear me?" he shouted.

"Ay—well enough."

"I'm facing you with going through a tunnel of Rats."

Bloggs waited a moment for a reaction, but no-one spoke.

"I'll be fair—these be not ordinary rats but big, hungry Rats. Is that right, Dingle?"

"Man-eaters," muttered Dingle.

"Ay—man-eaters says Dingle and he knows. Now, we don't know what's t'other end of Pit, because by rights the Canallers should've dealt with aforesaid Rats and as I see it, they 'ave not. Why, I don't know and nor can I hazard a guess, as is said. All I know is the Maps, and I know that t'other side of Grue's Pit is Beasley's Arches, and that's where we all want to get to. So either we goes on or we goes back to Long Shaft to sit it out for another four year or whatever.

"Now you all knows how we run things between us, and that is with everything fair and above-board. Bodger! 'Ave I been fair?"

"Ay, Bloggs, fair you 'ave been."

"Right. If anyone wants to go back there's no blame. Speak up."

There was a general muttering: "Rats is bad, but we got our shovels."

"I'm for not going—I votes we go back and 'ave a Conference."

"No—we're here now—let's go on and bash 'em."

"They ruined our Bridge—how much more do we have to take?"

"Drive fast enough, Bloggs, and them Rats don't stand a chance."

"I 'ave to say one more thing, men," shouted Bloggs, "And that is this. When I hits this 'ere wall, I'll be driving fast. Fast enough, I 'opes, to breach it. But once I've hit it, that wall slows me up and I'll need fifteen seconds at least to get up speed again. That's when them Rats gets their chance."

"Rats is only rats."

"Ay, but millions of 'em."

"Can't kill us."

"Enough of this, men. We can't talk for ever. Ay or no?"

"Ay," came a big shout.

"Right; then we'll do it proper, 'cos when we break out into Beasley's Arches we've gotter make sure we're going to *win*. In other words, we'll take the Arches like we took Long Shaft—not just by bashing 'em, although we'll do that, but by using our brains as well.

"Now I don't know what to expect there but I do know one thing, and that is that they're not expecting *us*. Not since that Bridge went down, they're not. So the first charge will be the vital one and I want everyone in on it, including the Passenger Coach men. Go for 'em hell for leather, but if they looks like getting the better of us I shall pull the Whistle. I shall only pull it if I has to, but if you hears it, obey it—get back to the train and keep your rear covered, and no mucking. Any questions?"

"No—on to Beasley's and bash 'em," came the shout.

"Right—Bodger? Tap that wall."

Bodger grabbed a pickaxe and gave a cautious tap.

"How is it, Bodger?"

"Thin, Bloggs," and they all heard the harsh squeaks.

"Tap it all over, Bodger."

"I 'ave now tapped it the 'eight and width of the train,"

said Bodger with dignity.

"Then everyone back to the trucks. Them who is fortunate enough to 'ave tarpaulins, pull 'em over and fasten 'em. The Widgie-boy stays up 'ere with me. You says you don't mind Rats and I do—I hates 'em. So now's your chance to do something useful—you fights 'em off me while I drive."

"I wouldn't *fight* them," said Widgie seriously.

"Well, whatever you'd do with 'em *do* it," said Bloggs fiercely, "because I'm going to be what's called occupied. Grattle take that Jumper back to the Guard's Van and stand over 'im with a shovel. Bodger—"

"I 'ave a request, Bloggs," said Jumper quickly.

"Ay?"

"That I be let go to make me way back to Long Shaft. I've done me job for you Bloggs, and seeing as I ain't a Railwayman I don't see why I should have to face them Rats. Also, when you lot gets to Beasley's, what d'ye think I'm going to do? Fight me own kind? 'Course not. I'll turn round and fight you lot, won't I? Stands to reason."

"He's right, Bloggs," said Bodger. "Let 'im go, I say. We don't need 'im now."

Bloggs looked thoughtfully at Jumper.

"Not so fast, Jumper-me-lad. Just you answer me a question before we decides whether you comes or no. What happens t'other end of Grue's Pit, Jumper? You're a Canaller—you should know."

"I *don't* know, Bloggs and that's the truth. I be from Long Shaft and I only went to Beasley's once in me life when I was a young 'un. I don't even know where Grue's Pit comes out. I ain't yer Dingle, Bloggs—I don't *know*."

"Be you sure, Jumper?"

"Ay Bloggs—if I knew I'd tell you, just to get back to Long Shaft again, but I don't."

Bloggs looked hard at him, then at Bodger.

"It's no good, Bodger, I don't trust 'im. He might tell the whole of Long Shaft where we are—he might raise a

111

counter-attack from Shipley's. No—you comes with us, Jumper, and when we gets there you can do what you will. Get in the Van with Grattle, like I said."

Jumper looked as if he was going to jump at Bloggs, but then he changed his mind and turned quickly back to the Guard's Van. Bloggs watched him go uneasily, and then got down to business again.

"Bodger—like I was saying before this slight interruption— you be up 'ere in the cab with me, to stoke. Is all in the trucks?"

"Ay—all in."

Bloggs shouted down the line.

"Then keep yourselves down and your shovels up. I'm going to back down about half-a-mile and then make full steam ahead."

He whispered to Dingle: "Will you stay up 'ere with me?"

Dingle sighed heavily. "I've come this far, I s'pose I might as well. Ay."

"Tell me, Dingle—how long?"

"Should be two mile at most. But I don't know what we find t'other end."

"Meaning?".

"Canal Folk seem healthy enough."

"So—"

"Couldn't be with Rats."

Bloggs looked at him in silence, and then began reversing. At nearly a mile, he stopped.

"This is it," he muttered to himself. "Stoke up, Bodger. I want every ounce of steam you can give me."

The train gathered speed slowly.

"At least let's 'ope we gets through them rocks without a bust boiler," said Bloggs grimly, to himself.

* * *

Fillbreach had climbed the hill at the far end of the Arches to buy wood for the *Blisterlee's* new cabin. The wood merchant was called Winder, and he had his shop right at the base of the rock wall. Above it were the lighted windows of his bedrooms, where he lived with his very old and deaf assistant who helped him measure up and saw.

"Rats be excited tonight," said Winder, conversationally, to Fillbreach.

Fillbreach looked behind him at the blocked-up cave next to Winder's shop. There was a large sign painted across it: 'Danger—Grue's Pit.'

"Eh?" said the assistant.

"I said, Rats be excited," roared Winder at him, irritably.

"Eh?"

"He's a good measurer and sawer, though," said Winder tolerantly.

"Don't hear so good, though," said Fillbreach, paying for the wood.

"He hears alright on pay-days," grinned Winder.

Fillbreach walked thoughtfully back to the *Blisterlee* with the wood. He could hear the squeaking and scrabbling from Grue's Pit quite clearly.

"Wouldn't like to have that Winder's shop," he said when he got back to the boat. "All that squeaking right next to you."

"Don't trouble 'im," said Blister. "The wall's thick enough. *They* don't get out."

"Making a lot o' noise, though."

"Don't hear 'em, normal."

"Do tonight. 'Rats is excited tonight', Winder said."

"What's that?" said a sharp voice from behind them.

"Hallo, Cap'n. Come to see the Wreck of the *Blisterlee*? Winder said the Rats be noisy tonight."

"Are they, indeed?" The Captain looked puzzled and strolled up the hill to Winder's shop.

"Not usually like that, are they Winder?"

"Never, Cap'n. Can't hear 'em in the normal way."

The Captain turned round and surveyed the jetties as if

looking for someone. "Rattle! Where are you? Rattle—come up 'ere a minute."

Rattle was old, but bright as a button, and he ran up the hill like an agile little monkey.

"Ay, Cap'n?"

"Listen to them Rats. What are they on about, d'ye think?"

Rattle moved over to the big sign and put his ear against the blocked-up cave.

"Ay—they're proper worried, Cap'n. Worried but excited, I'd say."

"That's odd. When d'ye hear 'em like that last, Rattle?"

"Can't say I ever has, Cap'n. Not since they was first blocked up."

"Is the wall alright? Not thinning out or anything?"

"No—wall's the same—it's just them what is louder."

"I don't like it, Rattle. There's a reason for it somewhere."

Rattle scratched his head.

"Danged if I know what it could be, though, Cap'n."

From a long way off down Grue's Pit they heard a low rumble that went on for almost thirty seconds.

Rattle relaxed. "That's it, Cap'n. It's a rock-fall, and they sensed it coming. They're funny things—Rats."

"Listen, Rattle; I can hear their feet. They're rushing around fit to bust."

"That's what it is, though, Cap'n. Nought to worry about, just a—"

Rattle stopped in mid-sentence. He cocked his head on one side and listened intently, holding up his hand for silence.

He looked at the Captain. "Do you hear what I hear, Cap'n?"

They both listened, with their ears against the rocks.

Chuff. They stared at each other.

Chuff, chuff.

"I don't believe it—they wouldn't dare."

Chuff, chuff, chuff.

"But they have, Rattle, they have."

"They'll kill themselves. It's suicide—they wouldn't do that."

"Maybe they don't know this end's blocked up, Rattle," said the Captain with a tight smile.

The sounds from the train got louder and the clamour from the Rats grew louder with it.

"They're going fast," said Rattle, his face white.

"So are the Rats," said the Captain grimly.

Suddenly he hit the wall with his stick, in a frenzy.

"They're trapped," he shouted. "Like rats in a trap. The fools."

Rattle shuddered and turned away.

"They'll be eaten alive."

Chuff, chuff, chuff.

The noise could be heard all over the Arches now and all the men on the jetties stood motionless, as if frozen, looking up at Grue's Pit. They could hear the couplings clanking and the engine snorting. They could hear the wild clippety-clop of the wheels rushing faster and faster along the track, and now they could even hear the feverish squeaking, running and scrabbling of the Rats.

Chuff, chuff, chuff, chuff.

"Gawd," said Blister, turning pale. "The poor beggars can't get out."

The Captain and Rattle, Winder and his assistant, were backing down the slope with their hands over their ears. Some of the men on the jetties had turned away, looking white and sick.

Suddenly there was an enormous explosion.

Rocks flew high into the air and rained down on the Arches like a terrible rain, and then, like an awful, drunken old monster, belching fire and smoke, the front of the *Flying Blogger* lurched through the wall in a cloud of steam.

Boiling water spouted from its sides and it was bent and twisted into a strange shape like a malignant face. From behind it there came a thin and ragged shout, "The Railway," and then the Railwaymen appeared, scrambling through every gap in the broken wall.

There were hundreds of them and their hands and faces were stained with blood.

10

The Battle of Beasley's Arches

The Canallers shook themselves out of their stupefied horror, seized any weapon that was to hand and rushed up the slope towards Grue's Pit. A double fear clawed at their hearts—fear of the Railwaymen and fear of the Rats, whose red eyes were looking down on the battle from the ramparts of Grue's Pit as if they were the audience at a theatre.

The Railwaymen tore down the slope waving their shovels and pickaxes. Exhausted they were, but this was their moment, the moment for which they had endured everything. "Whack 'em, whack 'em," they shouted as they ran, and "The Bridge, the Bridge," they roared as they clashed with the Canallers rushing up.

What a clamour as shovel met boat-hook, as pick met oar. Two mediaeval armies clashing on a foreign field could not have held more fury nor met with more abandon. Wood splintered against iron and oars became spears, those disarmed and grounded groped to find new weapons and rose to fight again. Hand to hand they struggled, and the violent centre of the battle swayed stubbornly up and down and from side to side, for every inch given was an inch to be regained.

The Canallers held the Railwaymen for fully five minutes, but they were outnumbered and had been caught unready for battle. The Captain had seen that defeat on the slope was inevitable, and he had turned his back on the battle and half-run, half-limped down to the Arches. A dishevelled figure appeared at his side and he had raised his stick.

"Jumper from Long Shaft", it had gasped, and the Captain had felt himself seized and helped forward. Together they gained the Square and the Captain hobbled straight over to a huge, curved horn of bone that hung on the third arch.

The Horn of Mortal Danger had not been sounded since the Blocking of Grue's Pit, but is was a sound to which the Canallers knew only one answer:

"The Arches are threatened—defend to the death."

The Captain reached up and unhooked it, staggered beneath its weight, drew in his breath and blew one long powerful blast. The sound rolled round the Arches like the bellowing of an anguished bull—on and on it went, and when it stopped, its echoes were like a hidden herd answering from far away.

In the barrack-rooms beneath the Arches, in a hundred work-rooms beneath the barrack-rooms the call was heard and was answered, and, as the Railwaymen broke through the stubborn ranks and streamed down the slope towards the Arches, hundred upon hundred of Canallers were running up the twisting stairs beneath them, buckling on their belts and seizing weapons as they ran, in each man's mind a question mark, What is the Mortal Danger—what is expected of us?

The Captain saw the defence of the slope crumble and as he watched the Railwaymen hurtling down towards him, two thoughts jostled together in his mind: Can we hold them? and When will the Rats break out?

Bloggs had had no time for thought during the battle for the slope, but he heard the Horn as he led his men in their head-long rush for the Arches and he tried to grasp the situation. "Think Bloggs, think," he muttered. "Tactics—tactics—fighting is never enough." They had reached the square now and a quick look around convinced Bloggs that it was a death-trap. He stopped in mid-stride and turned to face his men.

"Form a Square, the Railway," he roared. "The next

attack will come soon and it may come from any of the Arches." He gave a sigh of relief as he saw that the men had heard him and had not yet lost their heads in the heat of battle. They formed up roughly into a big Square, for they were over two hundred strong, and they formed it only just in time, as the first Canallers emerged, blinking, into the bright light of the Arches. They looked about them for the Mortal Danger and they saw the grim Square of Railwaymen. "Attack now," shouted the Captain. "Attack now and from all sides," but they held back.

Bloggs watched them streaming out from both sides of the Arches and he watched those beaten on the slope running down to rejoin the battle, and his heart sank. How many more? he thought, and still they came up from the bowels of the earth, more and more of them, until they surrounded the Railwaymen in serried ranks twenty deep. Then there was a low rumble like distant thunder, rising to a shout:

"The Canal," and they hurled themselves forwards.

Bloggs threw caution to the winds. "Break out, the Railway," he shouted and the square became a turmoil of struggling bodies.

It was the moment Widgie has been waiting for. He had fought hard on the slope and had taken his place in the Square, but all the time he had been waiting for the fighting to become more confused so that he could slip away unnoticed to find Jen. "Careful though," he muttered to himself. "Do it gradually, and keep fighting."

The Captain wedged himself in the angle of one of the Arches and watched the battle with his one shrewd eye—his infirmity made him useless in battle, but he counted it an advantage to be left free to plan his tactics. At the moment, though, tactics as such were out of the question for the fighting was too widespread and disordered. He turned his attention to the broken ramparts of Grue's Pit and the Rats—everyone had forgotten them.

Their red eyes were still watching everything intently, but they hadn't left their territory—were they waiting for the outcome of the battle? How intelligent were they? Perhaps the lights held them back? The Captain shivered.

There was a sudden shout of triumph, and he pulled his mind back to the battlefield. The Railwaymen at the far end of the Arches near the jetties had won a major skirmish and were now sweeping up the square towards the slope. The Canallers there had been gaining the upper hand, but now they were forced to turn their rear and face the new attack. They began falling back towards the Northern Arches, where stood the Captain, and he decided to switch to a defensive strategy which he thought could be made to bite later.

"Retreat, the Canal," he shouted, at the top of his voice. "Cover your rear with the Northern Arches."

Isolated groups of Canallers managed to fall back, and those that had been fighting near the Southern Arches opposite began circling round so that they could join their comrades.

Bloggs saw what was happening, and he didn't like it at all. The Canal Folk far outnumbered the Railwaymen, and he saw their best chance in splitting up the Canallers into small groups. Also he didn't like the idea of the Railwaymen's rear being exposed to the Southern Arches. In the end, though, he decided to follow up the Canallers' retreat, for the boost that it would give to the Railwaymen's morale. He gave a rallying cry.

"Forward, the Railway. They've got their backs to the wall now."

At the same time he fell back to the rear rank. "Press forward but face backwards," he shouted. "Keep your eyes on them Southern Arches over there."

The Railwaymen were a disciplined bunch and they saw Bloggs' point; so, while the vanguard pressed forwards, the rearguard executed a turn about and advanced backwards, watching the Southern Arches warily.

Widgie had taken advantage of the circling movement towards the Northern Arches to work his way across to the jetty end of the battle. He was still fighting hard with the Railwaymen, who were now virtually herding the Canallers into the arcades behind the Arches, but now he had to make his first big move and slip behind the Canallers' ranks. There was an empty archway ahead—the last one before the jetties—and, with a quick look around, he darted behind it and stood there, his heart pounding. Ahead of him was a long, high corridor. There seemed no point in further hesitation—either he was seen or not—so he ran for it hell-for-leather and didn't stop until he was half-way along it. Everything was dimly-lit, and the noise of battle was distanced.

He looked back—no-one had followed him—and a wave of joyful triumph swept over him. There was a big wooden door on his left. He pushed up the latch and it opened. Thank goodness, he thought, and slipped through, shutting it after him. It led into a narrow corridor with a lantern in the middle of it, and more doors opened up on each side.

I must start calling Jen now, he thought. I can't help it if I'm heard, because she may be anywhere.

"Jen," he shouted, running down the corridor. "Jen!"

Up above, the Captain had noticed Bloggs' defensive action with the rear rank, and he grinned to himself. "Thank you, Bloggs—an excellent idea." He limped swiftly back to the Canallers' rear, looking for one of his second-in-commands. "Slyter," he shouted. "Back here."

A tough, square-looking Canaller dropped back out of the fighting. "Slyter—I want a hundred men, near enough, for a special mission. Tell 'em to fall out and come to me in Corridor Four."

Slyter nodded and ran back to the battle area, and the Captain waited. In twos and threes the men detached themselves from the battle and slipped back unobtrusively.

When the Captain judged he had a large enough detachment he spoke again.

"Listen carefully, for I'll not repeat anything. You are the Captain's Hundred, and the job I have for you will go down in the Legends. Leave here and go underground. Take the main passage to the Southern Arches—I'll give you a count of five hundred to get there, so go fast. Regroup there and wait in the shadows. *You must not be seen.* When you hear the Horn of Mortal Danger, that is your moment. Hurl yourselves at the enemy. You are but a hundred but make enough noise for five. Is that clear? Questions?"

"Can they hold out here without us?"

"They'll hold," said the Captain grimly. "Now go."

He limped back to the battle and shouted a new command.

"Give way, men. Orderly retreat. Give way twenty paces in all, but one at a time."

There was a triumphant shout from the Railwaymen as they felt the Canallers' line give a little. They pressed forward with all their strength, but Bloggs could see danger ahead.

"Steady, the Railway," he roared. "Don't press too hard," for he saw that if the Canallers retreated into the Arches—into their own mysterious territories—the Railwaymen would be lost in a rabbit-warren and open to outflanking movements from all sides.

But how could the Railway resist? How could they do other than advance? They had their foe on the run—were they to let them get away?

The Canallers were falling back, step by step, and for each step they took, the Railwaymen took another triumphant one forwards. Bloggs saw it was a trap, and he rushed up and down the lines like a madman. "Hold 'em, men. Don't let 'em get you in the Arches. We're lost if we have to fight in the Arches."

But he knew it was an impossible command.

"The Bridge! The Railway!" they roared as they pressed forwards.

The Captain's eye was gleaming with excitement.

"One pace at a time, men. Good—good. Slowly does it. Just one pace at a time—backwards . . . "

* * *

Widgie had made two left turns, one of twenty and one of thirty paces, and now here was a smaller tunnel to the right. Should he go straight on or turn down it? He shouted "Jen" again—not a sound. There's no knowing *where* to go, he thought. It's an absolute rabbits' warren.

Then, as he stood listening, he heard a tiny sound. He cocked an ear. It seemed to be a long way off and it was a sort of rushing noise. He waited, frozen in mid-stride, and it came a little nearer. It was the patter of feet, he decided —no, the *pounding* of feet far away.

Panic seized him. They must be after me. He could hear hundreds of feet now, getting louder and louder. They seemed to come from everywhere—behind him, in front of him, above and below him, even from the tunnel into which he'd been peering. He looked around in every direction, but he could see nothing except the tunnels and the lanterns, and yet the noise still got louder.

There's hundreds of them—they're everywhere. They're coming to get me. "Jen," he shouted uncontrollably. "Jen —Jen"; and he began running down the passage, and then anywhere. He ran as fast as he could, but the faster he ran the louder came the noise.

They're *all* after me, he thought as the hundreds of running feet became thousands, echoing from all sides and all ends. He couldn't decide where to turn—he ran into every opening he could find, he doubled back and redoubled back as if he was in a maze, and always the noise seemed to follow him. Another turn left—another right—there's another—I can't run any more, he thought desperately. They'll just have to get me.

He stopped running, and he had stopped near some steps going downwards. He took them, two at a time, and they went down and down and round and round in a spiral, and the farther down he went the fainter became the running feet. I'm winning, he thought, and still the steps went down and round until at last he reached the bottom and collapsed in a dizzy, gasping heap.

After a moment he looked up.

Everywhere was very silent and still, and in front of him was a blank, stone wall, dripping with moisture.

11

The Horn of Mortal Danger

After the Captain's Hundred had made their mad dash through the tunnels, they emerged, panting for breath, in the arcades behind the Southern Arches. They looked round at each other, mentally counting up their number.

"We're all here."

"Yes, but stay still."

"No—regroup quietly."

"Keep out of sight."

"Keep your voices down."

"Get your breath and wait—we've got a battle to win."

They crouched in the shadows and watched the fighting from their new vantage point.

"The Others are winning—they're pushing us back."

"That's because we're not there. Come on, Cap'n, hurry up and give us the signal."

"They'll push 'em back into the Arches soon. Forget the signal. Let's go now."

"Ay, let's charge now and get it over with."

"On peril of ye life, me boy."

"Ay, you wait for the Cap'n. He knows what he's up to."

But the Captain's mind was elsewhere; he was trying desperately to work something out.

He had been in the Canallers' rear, regulating their planned retreat, and then he had limped further down the line to assess the Railwaymen's position. He had seen Bloggs and he had heard his warning shouts to his men.

"No fool, that Bloggs," he had grinned to himself. "He sees the trap, but he can't stop 'em walking into it."

He edged a little higher up to get a view of the Southern Arches. They should be there by now—was that them, the darker shadow in the arcades? "Keep out of sight, the Captain's Hundred," he prayed.

He ran an experienced eye over the battlefield. Funny—there was something odd about it. Something was wrong. What was it? Concentrate. He studied every detail intently.

The Railwaymen were a good fifteen paces inside the Arches now, and were already looking cramped. All well there—give it five more paces and I'll give the signal.

Is that it? he thought suddenly, but the Horn was hanging in its usual place, where it should be. There *was* something wrong, though—he was sure of it. Something in the battlefield. Not the Railwaymen's rearguard. The vanguard, then. He moved round to get a better view, and then whatever it was began to crystalise in his mind.

He hobbled round to the Canallers' rear to look at the other side of the attack again. Then he climbed painfully up some metal stanchions in the wall, where he had a bird's-eye view. His eye flickered from one end of the Arches to the other.

You fool, he almost shouted to himself. He half-fell down the stanchions and limped, panic-stricken, round the battlefield.

"Bloggs—Bloggs," he shouted.

Where was he? He'd seen him only a few minutes ago trying to control the Railwaymen's advance—now he was nowhere to be seen. Perhaps he was fighting his way up to the vanguard to shout his warnings there. Yes, that must be it. Still shouting "Bloggs" at the top of his voice, the Captain plunged into the battle from the flank and tried to struggle forward to the Railwaymen's front line.

He was buffetted from all sides, as much by the boathooks of his own men as by the picks of the Railwaymen. He dodged and darted this way and that, but he couldn't avoid them all. A shovel caught him hard on the shoulder and he was down. He struggled to get up, but his stick was lost, panic grabbed him at the thought of being trampled and crushed underfoot. He groped wildly for the stick, found it, and hauled himself up painfully. A pickaxe hit the side of his face and he felt the warm blood trickling down his cheek. Panic and temper combined to madden him and he lashed out on all sides with his stick.

Where *was* Bloggs? We must act now and quickly. No time—

He fought his way out and half-ran, half-hobbled, round the back of the Canallers' lines to look for him on the other flank. He was terrified of entering the battle-area again, but he forced himself to do it, holding his stick up to protect his face. He felt a hard thud against his injured leg, and it gave way under him. He fell, dragged himself up, fell again. When he looked up he saw that he was at Bloggs' feet.

"Bloggs," he shouted, and grabbed his leg.

"Ho—the Captain, is it? You get no quarter from me, Cap'n. Say your prayers," and Bloggs lifted his shovel high above his head.

"Speech," screamed the Captain. "I claim the right of speech."

"'Surrender' is the only speech I'll hear from you, Cap'n."

Then Bloggs caught a glimpse of the Captain's bloody and distorted face.

He lowered his shovel and dragged the Captain violently to the edge of the battle.

"Alright, Cap'n. What d'ye want? It's only one word and it's quickly said—'Surrender'."

The Captain tried to get his breath, but he couldn't. He wiped his bloody face and tried to speak, but no words came.

"Spit it out if ye will, Cap'n, or let me get back to the

fight."

"The Boy—"

Bloggs stared. "What trick is this, fool?"

"The Boy from above. He's gone."

Bloggs looked around. "The Boy's fighting. Out of my way, cripple."

"Bloggs—I'm telling you hard facts. *The Boy's not there.* He's disappeared. No—don't look, I've done so. Either he's escaped or he's looking for the Girl. We can't let it happen, Bloggs, you know that. If they get away and up above it'll be the end of us. All of us."

Bloggs looked round with malevolent eyes.

"If it's true—if that Widgie-boy—I'll kill him, I swear I'll kill him." He broke off and pulled himself together. "Don't move from here. Wait for me."

He rushed off, rushed round the field of battle and in and out of the lines like a madman. When he came back there was a new expression on his face.

"You're right. We must act. The battle can be won later. This will have to be done now."

"Ay—won or lost, that's as maybe, but we'll both be losers if them two gets away. What think you, Bloggs—can we stop the fight?"

Bloggs looked at the seething mass of bodies on the battlefield and shook his head.

"That we cannot. They're in battle-lust now—nothing can stop them till one side or t'other wins."

"And yet—" The Captain looked helplessly at the struggle. He knew Bloggs was right. Had he himself not been nearly killed trying to exchange a word with Bloggs? The smell of battle was in their nostrils. He stared at them and then back at Bloggs and his gaze wandered vacantly as he tried to think. Slowly a new look came into his eye as it fell upon the third Arch.

He caught Bloggs' arm. "The Horn, Bloggs," and he pointed upwards to where the Horn of Mortal Danger hung.

Bloggs stared, uncomprehending.

"If I blow the Horn, they'll stop, Bloggs. I promise they'll stop—maybe only for a second, but they'll stop. Shout to them, then. You know how to shout—*tell* them Bloggs. You'll have five seconds to stop them before the battle-lust gets at them again. It's a chance, Bloggs—the Horn to stop my men and your shout to stop yours."

Bloggs remembered the Horn of Mortal Danger. He looked at the Captain.

"Go do it, then. There's no other hope."

The Captain held out a blood-stained hand. Bloggs hesitated, then took it.

"Do it now," he said.

The Captain limped over to the Horn. It was only twenty paces, but he was so drained that he thought he couldn't get there, let alone drag down its huge weight. He grasped it with both hands and looked at Bloggs.

Bloggs nodded.

The Captain drew a long painful breath and once again the wounded bull bellowed and once again the hidden herd echoed its answer.

The Canallers automatically checked themselves in mid-stride. What new Mortal Danger threatened, other than those they were already facing? And then, even before the sound died, and while the echoes still rolled, Bloggs spoke.

His voice rolled above it like the voice of Moses returned from the mountain. He didn't shout or roar—he boomed forth the voice of reason.

"I speak for all. Stop. Stop the fight. We are in Mortal Danger—I speak for all."

Bewildered Railwaymen slowly lowered their weapons—just as victory was within their grasp, was it to be snatched away? The Canallers knew that only the Captain had the Right of the Horn, yet there was something in Bloggs' voice—they slowly lowered their oars and billhooks and the battlefield became, for a moment, a silent armistice.

The still moment was torn by a wild shriek, and the shriek gave way to a high-pitched yelping, and the yelping to a hard and indivisible shout: "The Canal!"

Like a fierce wind sweeping down from the Southern Arches the Captain's Hundred charged.

It was a charge of unearthly ferocity, abandoned and deathly. It was invincible, made by men who were, for the moment, gods.

It was an event of utmost terror.

The charge tore into the Railwaymen's rearguard with an impact that destroyed it in a second, and the whole battle-field opened up like a gaping wound and crumbled.

Bloggs stared with wide and unbelieving eyes, and then he swung round on the Captain.

He was white, and trembling with uncontrollable fury.

He pointed a shaking and deadly finger.

"Traitor," he hissed.

And then, as if the bellow of the Horn had broken a hypnotic trance, the Rats crept forth from Grue's Pit.

They blinked their red eyes in the lamplight, and their nostrils were twitching.

12

The Deep Dungeon

Widgie looked at the wet, blank wall and a heavy stone lowered itself into his stomach. The thought of climbing all those stairs only to be recaptured again was too much for him. He remembered sadly all the excitement he and Jen had had exploring the Pit and the Railway and everything, but suddenly he felt too tired, and all he really wanted to do was stay where he was and go to sleep.

"Well, come in if you're going to," said Jen's voice irritably. "Don't just hang around."

Widgie raised his drooping head and stared round, open-mouthed.

"I said, 'Aren't you going to come in' whoever you are," said Jen's voice even more loudly and crossly.

"Jen," shouted Widgie, trembling all over with excitement.

"Widgie," screamed Jen in a totally different voice. "Where on earth are you?"

"I don't know. I'm at the bottom of a lot of steps but they don't lead anywhere, except to a blank wall. Where are you?"

"I'm locked up in a sort of dungeon. Oh Widgie—thank goodness you've found me, I didn't think you ever would"— she was almost sobbing with relief.

"Well, I don't know if I have *found* you," said Widgie cautiously, "but you sound quite near."

"So do you, but this place is so echoey that it's difficult to hear *where* you are. I mean, I heard your feet banging down the stairs but I couldn't tell where they came from properly. I thought you were one of the Canal Folk and I was going to throw my lantern at you when you came in."

"Good job I didn't come in then. Listen Jen, I'll try tapping this bit of wall," Widgie tapped the wet wall in front of him.

"That's my back wall," shouted Jen excitedly. "You're just behind my back wall. Can't you bash it down or something? They must have blocked up your steps to make my dungeon."

"Not a hope, Jen, it's far too solid. And I haven't anything to do it with, anyway."

"Well, you'll have to go another way round then. Listen, Widgie—outside my dungeon there's a rather stinky canal, and leading down to it is a long sloping corridor with lots of twists and turns, and before that there's two hundred and eighty-three steps in a spiral with six other dungeons at the bottom."

"It sounds very complicated," complained Widgie.

"Well it is, rather. Oh, and listen, the corridor bit is a hundred-and-twenty paces."

"I see," said Widgie, not seeing at all really. "Well, I'll do my best."

"You'll have to be careful not to be seen."

"You're telling me. There's hundreds of them upstairs all looking for me."

"Oh, how awful. But we've got to make it now we're so near. I'll keep shouting 'Hoy' to guide you."

So Widgie got up, feeling much better now, and started climbing up the steps again, and Jen's voice shouting 'Hoy' got fainter and fainter until at last he couldn't hear it any more at all.

I'm just as likely to lose her altogether in this place, he thought in a panic, running upstairs. What shall I do if I have to go right to the top? They're bound to get me then.

But it was alright—he didn't have to—because just round

the next spiral he found, to his joy, another set of steps leading downwards to his right. In fact, as he looked at them from above, he realized that it was a fork and that the spiral split into two at that point.

What an ass I am, he thought. I should have seen that. That's what comes of losing your head.

He set off down the other steps, hoping to goodness that they weren't another dead end, and started counting this time.

Although counting won't do much good because all I know is that there are two hundred-and-eighty-three from the top. Funny she didn't tell me about that fork.

Anyway, when he'd counted a hundred-and-twenty, the steps *did* come out somewhere—they weren't a dead end—in fact, they came out into a corridor, and there were the six dungeons Jen had told him about.

Now we're getting somewhere. All I need now is a sloping passage on the left.

But the trouble was, there were two of them—one to the left, and a bit further on was another going off to the right. He called out "Jen" a few times, but then he realized that that was no good, because he couldn't hear her 'Hoys'. He looked nervously over his shoulder—it felt very odd being alone in the middle of so many corridors with the lanterns making long shadows of his body.

What shall I do? he thought—toss for it?

Then he suddenly realized that it must be the one on the left because otherwise Jen would have passed it on her way to the one on the right and would have told him about it.

Unless she forgot, like she forgot to tell me about that fork. Oh, well, at least it's got a *bit* of sense to it, so he took the one on the left and started counting again.

It certainly twisted and turned a lot and kept on going down-hill, so this encouraged him, but then he got worried about the counting, because although he knew he had to count a hundred-and-twenty paces, that had also been the number of steps he'd counted from the fork. 'Did I get the directions wrong, I wonder?'

He started trotting, and then stopped. If I run I'll miss things, he thought, so he slowed down a bit, but not much, because he realized that although it all seemed very empty at present, it might become very full later on with lots of people who wanted to capture them both.

He was just counting "hundred-and-twelve" when the corridor took another turn and there was the canal, stinking away as Jen had said it would, and there were Jen's 'Hoys' coming through quite clearly.

"Where are you, Jen?"

"Here. Turn left," so he did and, sure enough, there was the door, but it had no grille in it, so he couldn't see in.

"I think I've got to you—are you there?"

"Yes, yes—can you open the lock?"

Widgie looked at the door and then at the lock. They were both very solid and old-fashioned looking.

"Not at the moment."

"Widgie—in the canal—can you see a boat?"

"A rowing-boat?"

"That's right—well it should have rowlocks to hold the oars."

"Wait a minute. Yes, it has. I've got one."

"Put it in the lock and see if you can turn it."

There was a silence while Widgie tried to turn a lock with a rowlock.

"Can't seem to," he said, still trying.

"Oh, there must be *some* way now that we've nearly got there."

Widgie stood back and looked at the door and thought. After a bit, he said, "Is that a light coming from under your door?"

"Yes—there's a lantern."

"*That's* the way," said Widgie.

"What do you mean."

"We'll *burn* it down, Jen. It's a wooden door."

"Of course—I didn't think. What's the best way?"

Widgie considered.

"What sort of lamp is it? Is it oil or wax or what?"

"It's oil, I think. At any rate I can hear liquid in it when I shake it. It's got a lighted taper sticking out of it."

"Right. Then all you've got to do is to get the oil out and onto the door without putting out the light."

"That's tricky. You know what I'm like when it comes to anything like that. All thumbs."

"Tell you what, Jen. Tear a bit off your jumper—or better, use your handkerchief—and dip it in the oil and then light it with the taper. As long as you keep *that* alight it won't matter if the taper goes out."

"Right. Give me a minute."

There was silence.

"When you've done that, Jen—"

"I have. It's burning beautifully. A bit fast, though."

"Right—quickly now. Taper out and spread the oil on the floor all along the bottom of the door. Fast, before whatever-it-is goes out."

Widgie saw oil seeping under the door.

"Light it," he said urgently.

There was a sort of *woompf* noise.

"Ow," said Jen.

"Is it alright?"

"I'll say it is and so was I, nearly. The wood doesn't seem to be catching, though. It's thick *and* its damp."

"It's *got* to," said Widgie to himself.

"It *is*, Widgie," came Jen's excited voice. "It's beginning to crackle," and then he saw the flames his side as well.

"Stand right back—it'll get jolly hot in there."

He watched the flames getting bigger and bigger and changing from red to yellow.

"Are you alright?" he said anxiously.

"Yes, but you were right about the heat. It's boiling."

"Alright. Look, I'm going to try to break it down with one of those oars."

He ran and got an oar from the boat and began banging it into the door where it was burning fiercest.

"Don't burn the oar; we may need it."

"O.K. There—I've got it through."

Jen saw the oar poking through, and then it disappeared and she heard Widgie banging away again. Lumps of burning wood began falling inwards and she could just see Widgie's jeans through the flames.

The oar appeared and disappeared several times in quick succession, and Jen retreated to the back of the dungeon in anticipation of the final collapse.

Suddenly there was a great crack as the hinges parted and the burning door fell inwards towards her. Jen gave an inadvertent shriek of terror and then dived through the flames, landing in Widgie's arms with such force that they both nearly fell into the canal.

"Oh, Widgie," she gasped, hugging him. "It's so good to see you again."

13

The Parliament
in the Great Hall

"'Ooray, 'ooray. The Battle of Beasley's won. Up the Canal," shouted the Canal Folk all at once, throwing their caps in the air.

Bloggs, still white and trembling, took two steps forward and hit the Captain full in the face, dragged him up and put both hands round his throat. They both staggered backwards to the Arches, the Captain trying desperately to release Bloggs' grip.

"Oy—get that Bloggs off our Cap'n," shouted someone, and half-a-dozen Canallers leapt forward and dragged Bloggs away. It took all their strength to hold him, for Bloggs was struggling like a man possessed.

The Captain pulled himself together and found his stick. There was a dazed and vacant look in his eye as the full realization of what had happened dawned on him, and as fact after fact marched slowly across his mind. He looked up slowly, and saw his men disarming the Railwaymen and fetching ropes to bind them, saw Bloggs finally pinioned on the ground, and saw the Horn of Mortal Danger, now silent and neglected, where he had left it in the arcades. He shook his head like a punch-drunk boxer and surveyed the bloody battlefield littered with broken weapons, and then his eye was drawn upwards towards Grue's Pit.

The whole slope was alive, as if someone was pouring endless black treacle down it.

"The Rats!" screamed the Captain, pointing.

Canallers and Railwaymen, both, looked up the slope,

and everyone became suddenly still as statues, victors and defeated united in a fearful horror. So quiet were the Arches now that they could hear the rustling as the Rats moved slowly towards them.

The Captain was the first to move. In a very strange and slow voice he spoke, and he moved backwards gently like a cat.

"No-one move fast. Move like the Rats are—slow and quiet like I'm talking. Keep your eyes on them. Back away slowly to the arcades, and then down the passages. Not one wounded body to be left. Bring your weapons. Make your way to the Great Hall. Shut every door we pass—no doors left open. Show the Railwaymen the way. Remember— slow and quiet and shut all doors."

As in a dream they backed away and it was as if every movement was a pain. They felt their way with their hands and kept their eyes, unblinking, on the Rats, and for every step they retreated, by precisely that distance did the Rats advance.

No noise but the shuffle of feet as they backed into the arcades and down the wide passages. Silently they opened the doors into the guardrooms and they wanted to run, but resisted.

Through the guardrooms and out through the far doors they shuffled, and as they entered the Curved Galleries they looked at each other and asked a silent question, for they had heard the outer doors into the guardroom shutting.

Are we all in and are *they* all out?

Some began to move faster, but "Sshh" said others, and the slow retreat continued through the Curved Galleries until they came finally to the doors to the Great Hall.

When the last man was in, the Great Doors were closed. No-one spoke but there was a sigh like the small wind before a storm breaks. Eyes were blinked again and minds frozen with fear began to thaw.

The Captain limped up to the Great Platform of Rock,

and climbed slowly up its stone steps. He seemed very small in that immense place, which was as high as it was wide and as wide as it was long. When he had reached the middle of the Great Platform, he sat himself down in the Chair of Judgement and looked round at the vast, silent assembly.

"Bloggs," he said wearily, and his voice sounded very old. "Will you come up here with me? We have much to decide."

"I don't decide nothing with traitors, Cap'n. I'll stay where I am."

The Captain's eye flashed with sudden fury, and he gripped the arms of the Judgement Chair until his hands were white. Then he stood up and leant heavily on his stick.

"Alright, Bloggs. It shall all be said."

He raised his voice high so that it rang all around the huge stone walls.

"Canallers—there is a score that must be put right. You did *not* win the Battle of Beasley's Arches. That is for the Records and for the Legends. The Captain's Hundred were called out in error. *My* error. That is also for the Records and the Legends. The Horn was blown for an Armistice in the face of a Mortal Danger and there is no blame that is not mine."

The Captain paused. "You all know who won the Battle for Beasley's Arches—they're out there now, taking possession." Then in a sudden passion, he shouted, "This is no traitor up here, Bloggs—this is only a fool."

He collapsed back onto the Chair of Judgement and the Great Hall was silent.

From the back there was a stir, and then the sound of a heavy tread. A pathway opened up through the assembly, and Bloggs walked slowly and deliberately the length of the Great Hall and climbed up the stone steps onto the Platform.

He stood there in silence for a moment while the Captain watched him, and when he eventually spoke, he spoke slowly and it seemed a great effort.

"I will say what was going to be said before the Charge that broke the Armistice." He paused, and there was an uncomfortable shuffling in the Hall.

"What I say is for all, Canal Folk and Railwaymen alike. The Boy from up above has escaped during the Battle." There was a hum of consternation. "That means, as I sees it, that he will look for the Girl. You have 'er here, Cap'n. Where is she?"

"Locked in the Deep Dungeon, Bloggs. He'll not find her there."

"That, Cap'n, I takes leave to doubt, on account of his astonishing pryingness." He raised his voice again for the men. "I don't 'ave need to tell you what 'appens if them two gets back Above-ground again. Ruin. Everything we've ever built'll be destroyed, just like our Bridge 'as been destroyed." He paused, to let his words sink in.

"Just like the *Flying Blogger's* been destroyed and just like them Rats is destroying your boats now. But if them two gets back it'll be everything—not even just the North London system but *everything*. Them Above-grounders'll come down and take us over, that's what they'll do.

"Let's keep our destructions to ourselves, I say. Am I right, Bodger?"

"Ay, could be you're right, Bloggs."

"If I *am* right, then, I says the first thing we does is we find them kids and bring 'em back. All of us together—the Canal and the Railway. You knows your systems and we knows ours and that means together we'll get 'em. Right, Bodger?"

"Ay, Bloggs, I don't disagree."

"Right, Railwaymen?"

"Ay," came a subdued shout.

"Cap'n?"

"Ay or nay, Canallers?" said the Captain, loud and clear.

"Ay."

"What about them Rats?" said a voice, stubbornly.

"Rats is something I don't proper understand," said Bloggs. "I call on the Cap'n to speak about Rats."

The Captain rose slowly from the Judgement Chair and limped to the front of the Great Platform.

"It's right that we should debate the Rats now, Bloggs, but I think it's little can be said. Rats is a mystery. We blocked 'em up in Grue's Pit when you lot turned 'em loose on us, that's all we saw of 'em. *You* know what they're like, Bloggs—you came through the Pit. But why was they just *creeping* down on us just now? That's not like Rats. And why did they *wait*? Why wasn't they straight at us when you bust the barrier? Why was it they was just sitting there, watching?"

"How far can they get?" said Bloggs abruptly.

"Now they're out they can get right through the system. They may be gnawing them outer doors down now for all I knows."

"If they gets right through the system, they'll be spread thin and we can deal with 'em."

"Maybe that's why they was creeping all in a bunch like that, in formation. Maybe they've learned their lesson."

"Ay, maybe," said Bloggs, "but if *you* don't know and *we* don't know, all we can do is deal with it as it comes."

"Then let's get back to them up-above people. If I may take it we is now a proper Parliament, I 'ave a proposal."

"I think we may take it we are," said Bloggs, interrupting, "but before you makes your proposal, Cap'n, I think you better make me and my men familiar with your Way Out passages in this 'ere Great Hall, because if, and I only say if, them Rats gnaws through all them doors, we'd better know where we're going. Also we needs to know anyways".

"Your point is took, Bloggs. Can all hear me?"

"Ay"—a deep rumble of voices.

"First, the way we came is not to be used for reasons obvious to all. On your right, men"—he pointed—"you will see a doorway to the New Canal on its way to King's Cross. We travel beneath you, but there's a communication to your King's Cross Line and thus to your loop that by-passes Beasley's.

"T'other side of Great Hall is that there archway—Camden Lock Line for you, Primrose Canal for us. That takes in your short cut from the Camden Line to Primrose Hill what I don't think you ever finished."

"Danged Camden-Lockers should've finished that months ago," muttered Bloggs to himself, looking at the ground.

"Them is the two main ways out. Behind this 'ere platform is a further door which takes us to our underground system, and links up with the Old Brecknock and the dungeons. I 'opes that is clear to all."

"Ay, clear enough. Railwaymen—is all clear?"

"Ay, clear enough."

"Then getting back to my proposal, Bloggs, it is as follows. I propose Great Hall here as Headquarters, with Bloggs and me in command. I further propose that when Bloggs and me, in mutual agreement, sends off a search party, it be Canallers and Railwaymen mixed, so there's always some as knows the Canals and some as knows the Railways."

"Ay," said Bloggs. "Do you agree, Bodger?"

"Ay, Bloggs, I agrees."

"I further propose we send off Runners—Runners to Shipley's Basin and Angel Basin and Runners to Long Shaft and King's Cross and anywhere where there be boats and engines. If we gets them Runners off fast we'll have the whole system alive within the hour, and them kids won't 'ave nowhere to hide. Not nowhere. I says Runners because your engine's bust and we can't get to our boats because of them Rats. Are you in agreement, Bloggs?"

"Ay, I am. But first let's get a party down to this 'ere Deep Dungeon. We need to know who we're chasing; and if the Girl's still there, we can use her as bait to catch the Boy."

"Ay, Bloggs—good. Blister! Where's Blister?"

"Here I be, Cap'n."

"Take a party of ten down to the Deep Dungeon and report back 'ere. If the Girl be still there, leave her there with a guard of five, hidden in case the Boy comes."

"What about Rats, Cap'n?"

"Listen, Blister—Rats we don't know about. We takes our chance—if it's ten Rats, fight 'em, if it's two million, run. Anyway, you'll be taking the Old Tunnel from here and that don't touch the Spirals till the Fork. I can't see them Rats gnawing down the door in the wide passage for no reason."

"Bodger," shouted Bloggs.

"Ay, Bloggs."

"Form up them groups like the Cap'n said. Ten to a group, all mixed."

"Ay, Bloggs."

"Jumper," shouted the Captain.

"Ay Cap'n," said Jumper, running up, but keeping well away from Bloggs.

"Get them Runners off. The fastest men we've got. *You* should know. Get 'em to Shipley's, King's Cross, Angel and the lot. Railwaymen as well for the stations—ask that Bodger who to pick. The message is 'All boats and engines out for two Above-grounders to be brought back 'ere.' And tell 'em to do it fast."

He turned to Bloggs, eye gleaming.

"It's another war, Bloggs—all of us against them two—I give it five hours at the outside."

Bloggs grinned.

"If you and me can work together proper, Cap'n, I'll give it three."

14

The Old Brecknock

Widgie disentangled himself from Jen's embrace. "We'd better get out of here before they find us and lock us both up."

"Yes, but which way? We must have a plan. We can't just keep running round in circles or they really will get us."

"I don't know—I haven't thought. Shall we try and get back to the Bump?"

"But that must be *miles*. Anyway, we don't even know which direction it's in. Can't we go down this stinky old canal and see where it leads?"

"No, of course not, because when they see the rowing-boat gone they'll know exactly what we've done."

"They will, won't they? Up the steps then?"

"I don't know about that either. If they brought *you* that way it must be their main route. I wish there was another way. Tell you what—let's just check out this quayside first. You go that way and I'll go this—but we'd better be quick, because they may come back any minute."

They ran off in opposite directions.

"Nothing," shouted Jen, when she'd reached the end.

"Nor up here."

They rejoined each other.

"Well, it had better be the steps after all. Maybe there's a turn-off we've missed, although I don't think there is. At any rate we mustn't go right to the top or they'll get us for sure. It's alive with people up there."

They started up the steps, two at a time, using their hands to steady themselves as they went round the spirals.

"Watch out for turn-offs," panted Widgie, who was behind.

They reached the fork and Jen stopped.

"There," she said excitedly pointing down.

"No—that was my dead-end."

"Oh. But look, there's a little archway in the wall about three steps down as well. Did you try that?"

"So there is—no, I missed it." Widgie went to have a look. "It's another spiral going upwards. The place is riddled with them. Come on, let's try it."

They started climbing again, only more slowly because it was quite narrow, but they'd only gone round two bends when they heard the clatter of running footsteps from far above them and coming nearer. They stared at each other in dismay.

"Which spiral are they coming down?" said Jen. "They all sound alike."

"I can't tell," said Widgie, listening. He ran back to the main spiral to listen there, but the feet sounded just as loud.

"It's no good, Jen, we can't risk it. We'll just *have* to go back and use the boat—it's the only way. Let me go first."

They fairly hurled themselves down the way they'd come, round and round until Jen thought she would fall with dizziness. They landed with a jump on the quayside again, and Widgie at once rushed to retrieve the oar and the rowlock from by the burnt door. He unwound the rope which moored the boat to the bollard on the quay, and held it while Jen jumped in.

She half-fell into the boat, which rocked so much it almost capsized, and then Widgie jumped in with his feet on both sides to steady it. He thrust the oars in the rowlocks.

"Which way?" said Jen, looking back fearfully at the spirals. "Do hurry—I can hear their boots again."

Widgie just rowed off the way the boat was facing, which

was towards what had been their left when they jumped in, and pulled on the oars for all he was worth.

"It's terribly heavy—I can hardly move it."

"It must be waterlogged or something. Pull harder, for goodness sake. It sounds as if they're almost on top of us."

The green slime on top of the water parted and the boat slowly got under way.

"How far's the tunnel?" Widgie had his back to the way they were going.

"About thirty feet, I think—pull *harder*."

Widgie pulled and pulled, using short, quick strokes, and the boat began moving a bit faster.

"Nearly there," said Jen, to encourage him. The footsteps were really very near now, and they could hear voices, although not well enough to tell what they were saying.

We'll never make it, thought Jen, and then suddenly they had, and were under the cover of the dim tunnel. Widgie took the boat in about fifty feet and then rested his oars.

"Why've you stopped?" asked Jen urgently.

"Sshh. Just listen—they can't see us here," whispered Widgie.

They waited a moment, listening to the boots getting nearer and nearer, and then they heard the voices quite clearly.

"They've got away. Look at that door."

"The varmints. They've burned our door."

"Not long ago, either. Look—it's still smouldering."

"Well that's that. Better get back and tell the Cap'n."

"Not so fast, Blister. Where've they gone? They didn't come up the Spirals."

"Could have done. Could've taken the dead end and waited till we'd passed."

"Or got past the fork before us and gone straight up."

"They'll get more than they bargained for if they did."

"Ay, that they will."

"Why don't you lot use your eyes? They didn't go up the spirals. Look at that water."

"Ye right. The Old Brecknock's awash."

"And there used to be a boat here. They've taken our boat."

"Which way though? Up or downstream?"

"Ain't no stream in Old Brecknock. She's stagnant. Blocked up both ends when Camden Lock Railway was built over 'er."

"Trust old Blister—'e knows everything. We've got 'em then, if she's blocked."

"Ay—we've got 'em."

"An' I know which way they went. See the way the slime's parted? They went up there to the left."

"Well done, Slyter. And not long gone by the looks. Let's get back and report."

"Let's take 'em ourselves."

"What—with no boat?"

"All we do is wait 'ere till they comes back."

"Oh—I takes yer meaning. No—what we'll do is we'll do both. Slyter—you waits 'ere with four of us, and the rest of us'll report to the Cap'n and come back with the row-boat from the Great Hall."

"What, down them spirals with a boat?"

"Ay, won't take no time with five of us. Slyter—you and your lot keep quiet and hide yourselves in Deep Dungeon. Then, if they comes back before we're here, jump 'em."

"Think it's just the Girl, or both, Blister?"

"Dunno, but with five of you, you should be able to take 'em. Anyway, we've got 'em caught like rats."

"Better than being caught *by* Rats, like us."

There was an uneasy laugh, and then the clatter of footsteps going up the spirals.

"Alright, men—leave that door where she is, so as they don't get no warning we're here, and then we keeps quiet and sits it out in Deep Dungeon. Don't move till we hears 'em getting out of the boat and then rush 'em."

There were a few more footsteps and then silence.

Widgie touched Jen's knee to attract her attention and gave her a soft "sshh". Then he lowered the oars in the water as though they were made of glass and very gently gave a couple of experimental strokes. There was scarce a sound, for the slime deadened the water, so Widgie took courage and rowed properly, albeit slowly and quietly. It was very dark and unpleasant, and as there was no rudder for Jen to operate, Widgie began to be worried about getting round the bends.

"Can you see, Jen?" he whispered.

"A bit—not far."

"Can you give me hand-signals when you see a bend coming up?"

"I'll do my best." Jen peered ahead. "It's just that it's difficult to see how far it's curving."

After a bit, she said, "I don't see the point of going down here if it's blocked up."

"Well, can you think of anywhere else to go?" whispered Widgie.

Jen thought very hard to see if another plan came to mind, but it didn't.

"What about that railway they said was built over the canal. Maybe there's a bridge or something we can climb up."

"That's why I'm rowing to the end."

"Oh." Even though he was whispering, Jen could tell he was irritated. Suddenly there was a violent scrape as the bows hit the side, and Widgie's oar was thrust violently forward. He pulled it in and pushed off into mid-stream with it. "Hand signals," he whispered crossly.

"Sorry," Widgie looked over his shoulder and negotiated the bend by shipping his right oar and rowing with the left.

"Widgie—if there *is* a bridge or something, and if it's in the other direction, past the dungeon, we shan't be able to get to it."

"I know," he grunted.

"That was funny what they said about the rats catching *them*. I didn't understand that bit."

"Of course, you don't know about the Rats—the man-eaters, I mean."

"No I don't, thank goodness. They sound horrid."

"They were rather. Hey—watch out, we're scraping again."

"Well it's not my fault this time. There's no bends yet."

"That's funny—it *is* scraping. I can't seem to move it. What—I know; we're scraping bottom. The water's drying up."

He bent over the side and put his hand in the water to feel the depth, and the boat tipped over alarmingly. They both clung to the sides and looked blankly at each other.

"There's only about a foot of water there, Jen. We'll have to get out and wade."

"What—in that slime?"

"It's the only way. We can't just sit here, and we can't go back."

"I s'pose it is. Alright—give me a hand over the side. I bet the bottom's slippery."

Widgie held out a hand and helped her into the water.

"Ugh! It's cold, too."

Widgie got out after her and they both started paddling cautiously up the canal. They hung on to each other because the canal-bed *was* slippery, but after about a hundred yards they noticed the water getting shallower, and not far after that it dried up altogether, leaving them walking on rough stone.

Widgie heaved a sigh of relief. "Well, that's better any-way."

"I wonder why it dried up?"

"I think if it's stagnant it just does. Probably in ten years there won't be any water at all."

"It stinks much less dried up anyway. I hope there aren't any of your man-eater rats down here."

"Of course there aren't," said Widgie, hoping he was right.

They were walking round a large bend now, and it seemed as if the tunnel was completely changing direction and also getting a bit airier.

It's the sort of place where there might be a fork, thought Widgie, but there didn't seem to be one and by the time it had straightened out he calculated that they must have almost completed a right angle turn.

"Look, a patch of daylight." Jen pointed ahead. "It must be a ventilation shaft. What a relief."

She began trotting towards it, and Widgie was reminded of the last time that that had happened, what seemed like ages ago, at Long Shaft Station. He watched her, silhouetted against the light, looking up and sniffing hard, and he followed at a more sober pace.

"No ladder is there, Jen?"

"No—we can't possibly climb up. It's the usual kind; wide at the bottom and getting narrower and curving on its way up. Isn't it awful to think of the real world at the top of it and we can't get to it? We need someone with a rope."

"Come on, we can't hang around. They'll be after us soon."

He dragged her away from it, but just as they were starting to hurry on they saw something large and dark looming up about twenty feet away. It seemed to take up the whole tunnel. They slowed up and crept forward cautiously.

"Oh, Widgie, it's a wall. It's where it's blocked up."

They stood in front of it and looked up at it in dismay.

"Well, that's it, isn't it," said Widgie, bitterly. "I s'pose we should have known it. They said it was blocked up and it is."

He gave the stone wall a vicious kick.

"Ow," he said, and Jen could hear that he was nearly crying from rage and despair.

"Never mind, we'll think of something. We always do. At the worst, we can go and have a fight with Slyter or whatever-he's-called in the dungeon."

"Yes, him and four others, and by the time we get there they'll all be there, too."

"Well maybe we missed a turn-off on the way here. They have little things called communication canals that are just big enough for a rowing-boat. Let's go back and look."

"It's no good. By the time we got back to the boat and then started rowing slowly enough to look properly, they'd have caught us. Honestly, I think we're sunk."

"We can't be sunk with no water," said Jen, making a feeble attempt to cheer him up. "Come on—let's have a look at this wall."

"It won't work, Jen. I know these walls—it took ten men ages and ages even to thin one out back at Grue's Pit."

"Oh, come on—cheer up, for goodness sake. At least, let's have a *look* at it." Jen was getting fed-up with Widgie's despondency, so she started examining it herself, and at last, having given it a few more kicks, Widgie joined her in a sulky sort of way.

"It's just a dry-stone wall," said Jen. "Look—there's no mortar or cement or anything. I don't see why we can't make a start on it—it's better than just waiting, and if we can find even one small stone and get that out, it'll help us get a purchase on the bigger ones."

"It's the *thickness*," said Widgie stubbornly.

Jen ignored him and began wrestling with a stone that at least looked a bit smaller than the rest.

"It's no good doing it in the middle," said Widgie. "They'll just fall down from above all the time. You've got to do it from the top, where the roof is—at least it's solid there."

"How do we reach them though?" asked Jen, much cheered that he seemed to be returning to his old self.

"By standing on each other's shoulders, of course. It means only one of us can work at a time, but I bet it'll be tiring work, and we'll need a rest in between goes."

"Of course," said Jen enthusiastically. "Come on—help me up—I'll go first."

So Widgie lifted her up by cupping together his two hands to make a step, and Jen, by using the wall as a support, managed to get herself on top of his shoulders.

"Hey—they're much smaller up here. I expect they had to find stones to fit the curve of the roof. Watch out—I'm beginning to chuck them down."

"Ow, that was my foot," said Widgie. "Throw them farther back."

After five minutes, Jen said, "It *is* thick, isn't it? I've cleared a hole wide enough for us, and about a foot deep, but there's no sign of it ending. Would you like to have a go?"

So they reversed positions, and Widgie saw that she had indeed cleared quite a big hole. The only trouble was that he was having difficulty in reaching the back of it with enough strength to drag any more stones out. After a few minutes, he was forced to hoist himself up *into* the hole and slide the stones out behind him, which slowed things up a good deal, but eventually he was able to lie with his whole body in it.

I must be three feet in already and no sign of the other side, he thought, and then shouted "Are you alright down there, Jen?"

"Yes; but hurry up—I'm sure they'll be here soon. I've got a feeling."

"Can't hear you," came Widgie's muffled voice.

She could only see half his legs sticking out now, but she could tell by the way they were wiggling about that he must be putting a lot of exertion into his work at the rock-face.

In fact, he was now so far in that he was having trouble

getting the rocks out, and he decided to let them build up behind him for a bit, and then give them an almighty kick.

Meanwhile, Jen's feeling was getting worse. She had no idea how long it was since they'd left the quayside, nor any idea how long it would take the Canallers to go up wherever they were going and get a boat down the spirals. What would happen if they arrived with Widgie in the hole and her out of it? She tried jumping up to attract his attention by banging his feet, but she couldn't reach them. Then they disappeared altogether as he hoisted himself even further in.

She suddenly felt totally alone and unprotected, so she started trying to climb the wall to see how he was getting on, but although she could get her feet into the cracks, she couldn't seem to find anywhere for her fingers.

She jumped back again, and just as she did so, she heard Widgie's still muffled voice. "Watch out, Jen," and a whole heap of rocks fell down almost on top of her, followed by Widgie's legs.

"Look out—I'm going to jump," they said, and then the whole of Widgie followed them.

"I've got through," he panted, brushing rock-dust off himself.

"Widgie," she shrieked joyfully.

"Sshh. Yes, I know, but there's a huge iron door or plate or something the other end, right over the opening. *I* can't get it down—I've tried. I'm just too pooped. Do you think you could have a go? I think it's impossible, but . . ."

"Of course." To Jen anything was better than that awful waiting. "Hoist me up."

Widgie got her on his shoulders, and she began squirming through what seemed now quite a long tunnel. At the far end she found the big iron plate—she hit it and it made a deep, booming sound.

It's very thick, she thought. Oh well, it's got to be bolted into the wall or something, and if the bolts are weak

I suppose there's a chance.

So she began shoving against it with her shoulder and pushing it with her hands, and then she loosened a large rock and started attacking it with that. It made a dreadful noise, and she wondered fearfully if it would travel back through the hole and up the canal to the quayside, but she carried on because there was no other way out. After a couple of minutes the noise changed somewhat to a lower note and she had the impression that it might be loosening; and then, quite suddenly, the whole thing tore itself away from the wall and collapsed away from her.

She watched, fascinated, as it fell—a great iron plate the size of the wall—fell backwards and crashed and clanged onto the floor like a huge cracked bell being tolled. When it came to rest, the sound still echoed all around her as if it had fallen in a cathedral, and when Jen poked her head through the hole she realized why.

The other side of the wall was an immense cavern, so high that she couldn't see the roof. It was bathed in dim light, from an unseen ventilation shaft, she supposed, and crossing if from one side to the other at a height of about fifty feet was the outline, dimly seen, of a huge iron structure with its feet in the dried-up canal. It was the Camden Lock Railway Bridge.

"We've found it, Widgie," whispered Jen in a frightened voice, but of course he couldn't hear her.

15

The Great Chase

"So I reckon we've got 'em, Cap'n, like rats in a trap."

"Ay, good work, Blister—do as you said and get the row-boat down there, and make it sharpish."

Bloggs looked up from the table where he had spread out a large map.

"One moment, Cap'n, if I may interpose."

"Ay, Bloggs—you know it's a Joint Command."

"This 'ere Canal—what's it called? The Old Brecknock?"

"Ay, Bloggs, that's right. The Old Brecknock—been soundly blocked these last twenty year."

"And beggin' ye pardon, Cap'n, you're taking a *row-boat* down there? How many does she hold?"

Blister, suspecting his plan was being undermined, nipped in quickly. "She holds four, right and proper, Bloggs, but we're taking five."

"You're taking five, are you Blister?" said Bloggs, with heavy sarcasm lightly veiled. He turned to the Captain and banged the map. "But our Camden Lock Line goes right over your Old Brecknock, Cap'n. Remember the place well, I do—a nasty stagnant bit of water till it dried up. Terrible whiff we used to get when we crossed it."

"Ay Bloggs, we all know about the Camden Lock Line being built over us at the Old Brecknock." The Captain banged the map as well. "But I don't quite take your meaning, Bloggs."

"The Bridge, Cap'n, that's what I mean. If them kids get up that Bridge they're out onto one of our main lines.

Five men'll be useless. That Bridge links up Long Shaft to Kings Cross, or did till you busted our Bridge over the Fleet. It's got sidings and branch lines and all sorts. Once they get on that line they're out of trouble. Leastways we'll have a job finding 'em. *Twenty* men won't be enough. *That's* me meaning, Cap'n."

The Captain smiled patiently and patted Bloggs friendly-like on the arm.

"I thought you knew, Bloggs, I thought you knew. When I say Old Brecknock is blocked, I mean it's blocked *before* the bridge, as well as *after* it. That's why we blocked it Bloggs, if you'll forgive the directness—as a bit o' protection after you built the bridge over us. That's why the water's dried up, Bloggs. Them kids can't get near your bridge unless they 'appens to have some gun-powder to blast down our wall, which, beggin' your pardon, I don't think they do 'ave."

Bloggs was taken aback, but it only made him the more determined.

"With respect, Cap'n, and I trust you'll take this in the spirit it's intended, I don't trust your wall—not where them kids is concerned. Remarkable instinct for survival, them kids have, and prying with it. In your own words, Cap'n, if I may make so bold as to quote you, that wall was put up near twenty year ago, and I doubt me if I'm not right that it ain't been repaired or looked at since. No, Cap'n—Joint Command is Joint Command, and I want as many men up that Old Brecknock as we can get, so that if them kids *has* made monkeys of us both, there's plenty to spread out in all directions and grab 'em."

"I don't think ye need worry about our wall, Bloggs," said the Captain sharply. "Repaired or not repaired, when we builds a wall, we builds a good one, though I don't belabour the point. What I do say, and what you appear to have overlooked, Bloggs, is that we sent Runners out to King's Cross not fifteen minutes ago, and I'm assuming your

lot'll have an engine out along that stretch within the hour.
Moreover and notwithstanding, we sent Runners to Camden
Lock Station simultaneous, and if your men don't 'ang
around, *they'll* have an engine out, and we catch 'em both
ways."

"All true and fair enough and no criticism of your wall
intended, Cap'n, but I *still* wants as many men as we can get
up that canal. 'No stone uncovered' is my motto, Cap'n.
What's the trouble? Don't we 'ave a bigger boat available?"

The Captain sighed and tapped his stick on the ground.

"Where's the Long Boat, Blister?"

"Curved Galleries, Cap'n."

"Grattle! Call Grattle, someone."

He waited, still tapping his stick.

"Ho—Grattle. Where are them Rats? Is the lookout
still posted?"

"Ay Cap'n. Rats be still in the wide passages. Seems like
they 'aven't got the hang of the doors yet."

"What d'ye think, Blister? Can ye get the Long Boat
down them spirals?"

"Doubt it, Cap'n," said Blister, looking malevolently at
Bloggs.

"Try," said the Captain, shortly. "What about draught?
Does she draw too much water for Old Brecknock?"

"No trouble there, Cap'n—just means we 'ave to wade a
bit further."

"Right—you heard what Bloggs said. Get as many men in
her as she'll safely hold and get 'er down fast. Oh, and take
that Jumper with you—he'll be useful if you has to climb,
which I takes leave to doubt."

"And don't forget to make it a mixed company—Railwaymen as well as Canallers—like we agreed," put in Bloggs. He
turned again to the Captain. "I 'as another point, Cap'n. We
still don't know if it's the both of 'em or just the Girl in
that boat."

The Captain made as if to interrupt but Bloggs held

up a hand.

"We don't *know*, Cap'n, we only *thinks*. So, bearing in mind me motto, may we 'ave a party of Canallers to cover every hidey-hole, passage, spiral and what-have-you under this 'ere Great Hall? Not forgetting your Curved Galleries and anywhere the Rats ain't. I wouldn't like us to catch the Girl and let the Boy get away."

The Captain was beginning to look a little worn. He caught sight of Winder sitting on the edge of the platform carving a piece of wood.

"Winder—you heard what Bloggs said. Choose yourself a party of fifteen and check all the Underground Passages for the Boy, and don't miss one cranny or you'll have Bloggs here after you."

Bloggs grinned. "Well, I think that's covered everything for the moment, Cap'n."

"Be you sure, Bloggs? Because I wouldn't wish to think we'd left a stone unturned, as ye might say yeself."

"As a matter o' fact, Cap'n, there *was* a thought came to me mind." The Captain looked at him with exaggerated politeness. "D'ye think them Rats could cut the Kings Cross—Camden Lock Line?"

The Captain's whole expression changed. He limped over to the table and stared at the map, not as though he was examining it, but for something to look at.

"The same thought 'as been with me too, Bloggs, but you didn't leave me much time to get it out. Me answer is, I don't rightly know but I doubts it. That line ain't like the Old Grue's Pit line—that line runs *over* the Arches with tunnel links down to this Great Hall 'ere. If they gets into Great Hall maybe they could, but I'll tell you something, Bloggs—I've got a funny feeling about them Rats.

"I think they're more interested in us than your blankety Railway Lines, no offence intended."

* * *

When Widgie heard Jen hammering at the iron plate, he began to get agitated. The noise was echoing right down the canal, and there seemed no way that it could avoid being heard back at the dungeon.

He hopped from one leg to another.

Oh, you ass, what are you doing, he thought. If they hear you they won't wait in the dungeon any more—they'll come rushing down on us. No, of course, they can't—they've got to wait for the boat. Or could they? I wonder how deep the canal is?

He wrung his hands in anxiety. "Stop it, Jen," he shouted at last, but of course she couldn't hear him. Then the noise got lower and suddenly there was an enormous crash. Widgie stopped wringing his hands, and a wave of elation swept over him.

She's done it, he thought triumphantly.

There was silence after the echoes had died away, and it went on for quite a long while; so long in fact that Widgie began to worry again.

"Jen?" he called, but although there was no answer, he heard the sound of scrabbling, and a little later her face poked out at him, looking frightened.

"Sorry about the noise, but I couldn't have done it any other way. I had to use a rock. Anyway, we're through, and you should see it the other side. We've found the Bridge, by the way. Here, can you reach my hand and I'll haul you up."

The hauling up bit was alright, but they got in a terrible muddle at the top, what with Jen trying to back down feet-first and Widgie trying to climb in headfirst. They managed it in the end, though, and there they were safely in the hole with Jen's legs dangling down one side and Widgie's the other.

"What a pair we must look," said Jen to Widgie's nose, which was only inches away from her. "Anyway, the only way I can think of getting down the other side is to feel for cracks in the stones with my feet, and then drop when I can't hang on any longer."

"And break your ankle. No—wait for me to follow you up, and I'll lower you down by your arms as far as I can, and then it won't be such a drop."

So in the end, that's what they did. Jen only had about six feet to drop and landed quite safely, but for Widgie it was another matter. First of all he had to turn himself right round and get his feet where his head was, exactly as Jen had had to do when she came back to fetch him, and this proved far from easy. However, Jen helped him with advice, and finally there he was in position.

"How far is it, Jen?" he called over his shoulder.

"About fifteen feet—it's deeper this side than the other, and it's rough ground at the bottom. But I'll try to catch you, so don't worry."

"Thanks," said Widgie to himself, and began finding toe-holds and trying to keep his hands from slipping. When he knew he couldn't hold on any longer he shouted, "I'm dropping," and Jen held her hands out in a rather ineffectual way. They ended up on the ground in a tangled heap.

"Strewth," said Widgie as they picked themselves up. He was looking up, awestruck, at the invisible roof and the big iron bridge towering above them.

"I know," said Jen, standing close to him.

They climbed over towards the base of the pier on their right to have a look at it; and it really was climbing, because on this side of the wall the ground was a rough quarry of huge rocks dug up by the excavations, through which the canal bed wandered like a dried-up stream.

"What do you think?" asked Jen, as they looked up at the iron struts that criss-crossed from one side of the pier to the other.

"Difficult to say. There's plenty of light from some-where—I suppose there's a ventilation shaft somewhere in the roof. It looks strong enough to hold us, but we can't really see what happens at the top. There's a nasty over-hang though, where the span of the bridge joins the piers. How wide would you say that was?"

Jen shut one eye and squinted up. "About two feet?"

"Yes—well that's the tricky bit, and we can't see what there is to hang on to above it."

"Wait a minute, Widgie—let me see it from an angle." Jen climbed back as far as she could towards the wall, and then stood on a rock. "There's nothing—it's got no sides or anything."

"What about the big curved bit above the span—hasn't it got vertical bits down to the track? We could hoist ourselves up with those."

"No—they only start later. They're not over the piers at all."

"Well, that's what I mean—it's tricky."

Jen rejoined him. "Look. Let's forget the bridge and see what happens to the canal after this quarry bit."

"I'm sure it's got to be the bridge, Jen. I only meant it was tricky. You see, *I* think the canal has a really proper block-up further on. It was something they said back at the dungeon. If we had time to explore, I'd say yes, but as it is . . ."

He felt above him, and found a strut.

"Come on, Jen, let's try it. Just keep an eye on my movements and do the same, only mind my feet."

They started off, and it was rather like pictures Widgie had ·seen of people climbing rock-faces, except that there was no rope. Hands up to grasp a strut, feet up to where your hands had been a moment ago, hands up again and so on. As they got higher, the distance between the struts got smaller and they had to climb two at a time to avoid banging their knees.

Jen tried to follow Widgie's movements, but after a bit she found she couldn't do that and still see where her own hands and feet were going, so she just concentrated on herself and found she got on much better that way. She didn't dare look down, but she thought they must be well over half-way when she heard Widgie give a sudden yell of pain and found that one of his boots was banging on her head.

"Alright," she shouted. "I can get your foot back on the struts."

"It's not my foot, it's my hand—it's caught. One of the struts has come loose and banged down on it."

Jen winced for him. "Don't try to pull it away. I'll climb up next to you and hold you and then you can use your other hand to get it off. Wait a minute."

She scrambled up to Widgie's left-hand side and put her arm round his back.

"O.K. I'm quite secure and I can hold you if you leave go. Just make sure your feet are good and solid."

She could hear him grunting with pain, and then she felt his whole weight fall on her arm as he let go and tried to lift the broken strut.

"The trouble is," he panted, "it's fixed on the other end and it's like a spring. Like a mousetrap. Ow. I thought I had it then."

Jen's arm began aching, and then the ache became an intolerable burning right up to her sholder.

"I've nearly got it up," and she felt Widgie pressing back harder on her as he wrestled with it. There was another agonizing thirty seconds.

"Ow—done it," gasped Widgie.

Jen felt his weight come off her arm as he held onto the struts again, and she waved it about gratefully to let the blood back.

"Are you alright, now?" she said.

"Yes, except my fingers hurt dreadfully."

"They'll be alright. Move them about a lot." Widgie began climbing again, only more slowly now, with the distance between the struts getting ever smaller and smaller

until he banged his head on something and realized that
he'd got to the top.

"I'm there, Jen. I've just banged my head on the overhang."

"Can you get over, do you think?"

"I don't know. I'm trying to find a way. I think if I
can get a grip on something solid and then kick off with
my legs I might be able to do it."

There was silence while Widgie got his hands over the
edge.

"I can't do it. My right hand's too weak."

Jen pulled herself up level with him and bumped her
head as well.

"Let me have a go."

She felt around above her with one hand, and then
climbed a strut higher, bending her head back against the
overhang.

"I've got it—my hands are on the rails—solid as anything."

She began hauling herself slowly up, until her body was
bent right backwards.

Then they both heard a noise in the far distance.

Chuff.

Chuff, chuff.

Jen's first thought was for her hands.

"I'm coming back," she said urgently. "There's a train
coming."

Now it was Widgie's turn to wince. "Quick—I'll guide
your feet back again."

"No don't—my only grip's on the rail. It's the overhang
—I'll just fall straight back into the canal."

Widgie heard the panic in her voice.

"It's alright. I've got one hand to hold you when you let
go. Just grab anything you can find. *You must let go of
the rail*."

"I can't—I'd rather haul myself up."

Chuff—chuff, chuff, it was quite near now.

"You must," he said urgently. "I'm here—I'll hold you."

"No, I'm going up. I can't do it."

"LET GO," roared Widgie.

Jen could feel the rails vibrating but she didn't know how near the engine was. "It might be on top of me—my fingers—" and she let go.

She screamed as she began falling and her fingers scrabbled uselessly trying to find something to hold. Then they slipped off completely and she felt Widgie's arm against her thighs.

I'm going right over backwards, was her last thought, and then one of her outstretched arms found Widgie's head. She wrapped it round him and arched her body forwards and then Widgie's arm found her waist and pushed her inwards. "Oh, my fingers," she gasped as she found a strut.

Chuff, chuff, went the engine from King's Cross as it roared across the bridge. They both clung on for dear life while the bridge rocked violently under the weight of the engine, and then it was over.

They looked at each other and tried to get their breath back.

"It wasn't a train," panted Widgie. "Just an engine. That means they're *all* looking for us—they wouldn't send out just an engine otherwise."

"Well, they jolly well missed us then," said Jen with grim satisfaction, sucking her fingers. "Let's stay here for a bit. I'm all in, and neither of us have fingers to tackle that overhang now."

They wedged themselves between the struts as best they could and were just about to rest a moment when they heard voices from the other side of the wall.

"Where they gone then? They ain't 'ere."

"Use your eyes—they've made a hole up there."

"Varmints—they've made a hole in our wall."

"After 'em then, afore they gets up that bridge."

"You first, Jumper—time you got in a bit o' jumping

again or ye'll be getting out of practice."

* * *

"I'm not satisfied," said Bloggs crossly.

"Found another stone 'ave you, Bloggs?" The Captain grinned sarcastically.

"I'll thank you not to over-exercise your undoubted sarcasm, Cap'n," said Bloggs sharply, "and in answer to your question, yes I 'ave. We're not *doing* enough, Cap'n, and that's the long and the short of it."

"Now look 'ere Bloggs—we undertook to run this 'ere chase rational-like. Send out men as needed to plug gaps, but always with our main force here to cope with unexpecteds. That was agreed between us, Bloggs. I 'ave already given in over several what I might call fools' errands, Bloggs, but I insist, and it is a word I have not so far used, that our basic plan stays what it was when we made it."

"Alright Cap'n—look at this 'ere map," insisted Bloggs, who had spent the last quarter-hour marking it with chalk. "It's a good map—no complaints there. It's got all our main lines marked up good and clear and no errors, and it's got all your big canals ditto. But you know and I know there's a lot more that ain't marked. Raise yer eyebrows, if you will, but what about the King's Cross—Paddington extension? Eh? 'Tain't there. Never finished you may say, but tunnel's still there.

"What about the Primrose Hill—Kentish Town Link that got flooded afore 'twas finished? Ditto, if I may make so bold. Come to think of it, what about the Beasley's—Primrose Hill tunnel? Not that big yet, admitted, but big enough for them two kids to use."

The doors on the right of the Great Hall suddenly banged open and a Runner made his way swiftly up to the platform.

"King's Cross 'ave got an engine out, Cap'n. Should be on her way to Camden Lock by now."

So engrossed were they in their argument, that for a moment both Bloggs and the Captain regarded him blankly.

The Captain pulled himself together. "Well done, Flicker. You moved fast—did you see any—?"

"No, Cap'n, not one."

Bloggs had gone back to his map again, and now he suddenly stood up and thumped the table.

"Look, Cap'n—enough's enough. Delay over t'others if you will, and I think you're wrong, but I want another Runner up to Camden Lock and fast. If, and I only say if, Cap'n, them kids gets up that bridge before the King's Cross engine, I want the Beasley's—Primrose Hill tunnel blocked the far end."

"You want—you want, Bloggs. Alright—you be going beyond the bounds of reason, but you has as much right as me to issue orders. Bristle! Find the best Runner we've got—not Flicker here, he's all in—and have him go to Camden Lock. The Station. Tell 'em to send ten men and an engine to block the Primrose end of the Beasley's—Primrose Hill Link as fast as may be."

"No, Cap'n," put in Bloggs quickly. "One of ours—they knows the routes better. Fudge! You 'eard the orders. Get going and make sure them Camden Lockers do it quick."

There was a sudden commotion at the back of the Hall as the Great Doors were flung open wide. Grattle stood there with bleeding hands, squinting about him wildly.

"Bloggs," he shouted. "They've got into the Guard-rooms. We're trying to hold 'em back, but if you wants my opinion, it'll be the Curved Galleries next."

* * *

Widgie and Jen looked at each other hopelessly.

"They've got to get through the hole yet," said Jen.

"They'll be through any minute, Jen. It's no good—we've got to have another try. It's just that overhang that frightens me."

"*I'll* try," said Jen bravely. "My hands are better than yours."

"Not much, if at all," grinned Widgie. "No, it's my turn for the high jump this time—you do the back up."

He got to his feet, stretched his arms one after the other, and wiggled his fingers painfully. "Could be worse," he said, and climbed up a couple more struts until he was right under the overhang.

"You stay a bit lower, Jen, so that you can reach up properly and hold me if I slip. I'll try and get my hands on that rail of yours. How far in is it?"

"It can't be more than a foot, but it feels more in that position."

"Nothing else up there at all to grab?"

"Not that I could find."

The dim daylight suddenly changed to a yellow lantern-light that swung and threw long moving shadows all over the cavern.

"There they be."

"Up you go, Jumper."

"Ay, but follow fast—I can't tackle 'em on my own."

As Widgie and Jen looked down they saw the men climbing one by one through the hole and down the side, and with each new arrival the yellow light got brighter. They turned their eyes away, blinking and feeling dizzy. It's like being on the trapeze at a circus and they're the audience, thought Widgie.

"Hurry up, Widgie," said Jen nervously.

"Don't rush me. Once we move it'll be over in a flash, but I want to get my bearings first."

He looked up and tried to work it out. Feet as high as possible on struts so I'm almost on my back. Try to get my armpits on the edge of the overhang. Are my arms as long as Jen's? Once I've kicked off, how to haul up? I know, try a pendulum movement. O.K. Here goes.

"Jen, if you see me swinging from side to side don't

worry. I'm off now."

He reached up and got his hands on the overhang. Moved up one strut and got his elbows over it. Last one—he moved his feet up one more and found himself almost horizontal. Grope with right hand. Nothing. Strain forward—yes. Beautiful; a nice solid rail. Hold tight and left hand forward. Made it—now for it.

He kicked his feet off the struts and there was a shout of triumph from below.

"He's slipped."

"That's the last of 'im."

"Only the Girl now, Jumper."

Widgie's feet dangled over the abyss.

"All I've got to do is never let go the rail and I'm alright."

He began swinging his body from side to side, only a little at first but gradually increasing.

Not enough, he thought. More—make it swing more.

He used his legs in mid-air to jerk his body at a wider angle.

Oh, my hands. Hang on. Can't be for ever. Give it three more swings and then up. One—two—this is the one—three, and on his way back from three he jerked his whole body as high in the air as he could and felt his right knee land on the top of the overhang.

He threw his whole body upwards and forwards and let go his hands as he felt himself rolling and rolling over the track.

Quick—no time; I must get Jen up he thought.

He scrambled up and peered over the edge. He saw Jen's white face looking up. "He's nearly up," she said, sounding as if she was trying to control her voice. He looked further down and saw Jumper's grinning face as he scaled the struts, as agile as a monkey.

"O.K. No panic. One strut up and get your hands on the edge."

She climbed the one and he saw her right hand come over.

"Hold on. Just wave your left hand up and I'll grab it."

He braced himself and put his left foot behind the rail for purchase.

Jen waved her left hand towards him and he got it with his right.

"Help," she screamed, "He's got my ankle."

"Kick, Jen." He hauled on her left hand and felt the resistance.

"Kick off with your other foot," he shouted.

He saw her do it, saw Jumper pulled away from the struts by her weight, and then saw her hanging free as Jumper was forced to let go. Her right hand came off the overhang and Widgie grabbed it before it disappeared.

Now to haul her up. Keep left foot solid. Try not to scrape her too much. Head over, chest over—one more pull.

He fell over backwards and there was Jen rolling over onto the tracks.

"They're up and over," he heard the shout from below.

"Come on, Jen—they'll be up and over themselves soon."

"Can't—too puffed. Just one moment."

He stood over her and waited while she gasped for breath, and then he saw the first of Jumper's hands on the edge of the overhang.

"No more time, Jen." He went over and trod on Jumper's hand just to delay things, and it disappeared.

Jen pulled herself painfully to her feet and looked at him despairingly.

"Which way?"

"This way—the way the train went."

They staggered, more than ran, for the mouth of the tunnel at the far end of the bridge. They didn't even hear the shouts from below because their whole attention was focused on the dark tunnel ahead. As the blessed gloom enfolded them and the bright yellow lights from the cavern receded, Jen slowed down.

"Keep going," gasped Widgie. "They'll be after us in a minute."

"Can't."

"Must."

After the bright lights, there was no question of seeing where they were going—they just stumbled onwards in the darkness as fast as they could. The tunnel started going downhill, and they slowed a little so as not to fall. Behind them they heard a voice shouting.

"Jumper's got there," said Widgie grimly.

"I can't go on much longer, Widgie. Really."

"Must," panted Widgie, and on they stumbled. They came to a bend to the left and the tunnel levelled out and then began a slight incline.

Jen suddenly stopped dead.

"Jen," shouted Widgie, accusingly.

"No—listen."

He stopped talking and together they froze in the middle of the tracks.

From only a little way ahead they could hear the rattle of an engine, and beneath their feet the rails were vibrating. They looked down and there was only a single track.

* * *

"Camden Lock engine's out. She'll be at the bridge soon," panted the Runner. "Had to wait to let King's Cross train through, they said."

"Alright, Gimpel, you did good." The Captain smiled grimly at Bloggs. "The net's closing in, Bloggs. The plan's working, you mark me words."

From the passage to the spirals behind the platform they heard someone running, and Slyter appeared.

"Blister said to tell you Jumper and twenty men are on their way up the bridge," he said, out of breath.

Bloggs swung round in a fury.

"UP the bridge? UP the bridge, you said?" He looked at

the Captain with hard eyes. "'When we build a wall we build it good'? '*Gunpowder*, what they don't 'ave'? Was I right or wrong, Cap'n? Don't argy-bargy—just one word, that's all I want. Which was I, Cap'n?"

"They made an 'ole in the barrier," said Slyter, thoroughly frightened.

"They made an 'ole, Cap'n. You 'eard 'im. Made an 'ole in *your wall*. You'll thank me, Cap'n, I made you take ye long-boat out. You'll thank me I made you send a Runner to block up that Link. And, Cap'n, you'll thank me for a lot more before this campaign's out. From now on, *Mister* Captain, I take charge 'ere. You do as *I* say, and you can danged well tell your men that, too. Made an 'ole—"

There was a violent commotion outside the Great Doors— they were thrust open, and a ragged group of Canallers forced their way through.

The Captain and Bloggs looked up, startled—"They're coming," was all they heard and then the Great Doors shut with a great crash.

Grattle rushed up to Bloggs.

"We can't hold 'em, Bloggs. They bite through the bottoms of them doors like cheese. They didn't get the hang of it at first. Now they know. I tells you, Bloggs, they'll be in here next—they're in the Curved Galleries already, squeaking and scrabbling, ay, *and* biting. We've lost two men—don't stop me Bloggs—I'm telling you straight. It's the end of the Arches, for Canal and Railway alike. Tell 'em all to get out."

Grattle stopped, out of breath, and squinted round at the assembly.

The Captain looked at Bloggs and spoke quietly so that no-one should hear.

"I thanks you for your tirade, Bloggs, and I says only one thing and that quietly, for you to think about. Who let 'em out, Bloggs—who let 'em out?"

He allowed the words to hang in the silence that had

fallen over the Great Hall.

Bloggs looked at the Captain and the Captain looked at Bloggs, and Bloggs sighed.

"Alright, Cap'n. But now we have to keep the Command going. We can't separate and let the men panic, and Rats may be Rats, but we can't let them kids get Aboveground either. It's either Camden Lock or King's Cross we retreat to."

"Camden Lock, Bloggs. Let's get to the centre of things. King's Cross'll be cut off anyway if Rats hold Beasley's."

"It's not Rats *holding* Beasley's that worries me, Cap'n. It's where do they go from here?"

"D'ye agree or not, Bloggs? As you say, yeself, it's only one word I want."

"Ay."

The Captain turned to the men, and put both hands on his stick as he faced them.

"You all heard Railwayman Grattle. It's not a time for talk. Abandon the Arches and every man down the tunnels to Camden Lock."

Everyone took up the cry, "Down the tunnels to Camden," and it became a shout and then a roar, as if they wanted to drown the noise that came from the other side of the Great Doors.

"You and me sticks together, Bloggs," said the Captain. "Someone's got to issue orders and it might as well be both of us."

Bloggs grabbed the Captain's map, and the two of them waved the men forwards.

"Make your own way, men, but we all meet at Camden within the hour. You'll get your new orders there."

"Camden—Camden," and they poured like a flood down the tunnels that opened off the Great Hall.

The last man had disappeared. The Great Hall was silent and deserted.

A tiny snout poked its way through a newly-made hole in the Great Door and peered cautiously around.

16

The Final Retreat

"It's going to hit us," said Jen in a panic. They couldn't see the train yet, but they could hear it was going fast.

"Flatten yourself against the wall. It'll be O.K."

"They'll see us—let's lie down."

"No do as I say—lying down is too risky."

They both flattened themselves against the sooty brickwork and Widgie immediately disappeared. "Help," he shouted.

The engine's big reflector lamps appeared round a bend higher up the track.

"Widgie—where are you?" She felt a hand grab her ankle, and screamed.

"In here—quick."

She let herself be dragged down she knew not where, and a few seconds later the engine roared by, scattering sparks in all directions, driver and fireman both leaning out of the cab, staring ahead.

Widgie grabbed a bit of Jen's sweater.

"Come further in—it's a tunnel, I think."

They got off their hands and knees and ran down it, half doubled up because they didn't know how low the roof was.

"That's far enough, Widgie. *Please* let's rest."

"Not yet—wait for a bend. Don't forget Jumper and the others."

They stumbled on about another hundred yards and then the tunnel curved to the right.

"O.K., now we can have a rest."

They both collapsed on the floor and said nothing at all for several minutes while they got their breath back. Then they sat up and put their backs against the walls.

"Where are we?" asked Jen, peering into the darkness.

"I've no idea. I just flattened myself against the wall and fell flat on my back."

"It must be higher than we thought then. A proper tunnel in fact."

"It's got no rails though." Widgie felt with his hand over a rough, earth floor.

"It's just a long *cave*. There's no brickwork or anything. Only rock. I say, Widgie, how did that engine get through on a single track? It should've hit the other one going the other way."

"They have passing places. I saw lots of them. They have points and everything."

"Sshh." Jen held up a warning hand. From the main tunnel came the sound of running feet and then voices.

"That Camden Lock engine should've caught them."

"'Twas going too fast."

The footsteps stopped.

"Flash a glim down that tunnel."

Jen and Widgie shrank back as a thin yellow light reflected itself round the bend.

"They ain't there."

"Could be further in."

"No—they got no lamps. Wouldn't see this little 'ole without lamps." It was Blister's voice.

"If they ain't there why didn't Camden Lockers see 'em, then?"

"Reckon they just layed down and hid. Engines is no good for looking."

The feet started running again and gradually receded until they were heard no more.

"That was a near one," breathed Jen, rubbing earth

off herself.

They got up, and tried to feel where the roof might be, but although the tunnel was quite narrow—perhaps six feet across they reckoned—they couldn't touch the top, even if they stood on tip-toe.

Feeling easier than they had for a long while, they started walking in single file, Jen leading the way. There were no ventilation shafts to provide light so they had to go very slowly, with Jen slithering her feet as she walked in case there should be a pit or an obstacle in front. The curve began reversing itself and turning to the left.

"Has the feeling of a dead-end to me," said Jen speculatively.

"A bit long for a dead-end—I bet it leads somewhere."

"The curve's straightening out, and it's getting wet."

Their feet began squelching in thin mud and the walls, when they felt them, were oozing water.

"Careful, Jen, we may be coming to a canal or a lake or something."

The mud was getting deeper and water began dripping on them from the roof.

"Sloshy underfoot *and* raining," grumbled Jen. "Hey, watch out, there *is* a lake."

In fact, there wasn't, but it was certainly a subsidence. The ground began sloping downwards and the mud gave way to a thin layer of water, getting deeper the further forward they went. When it was up to their knees, Jen got a bit anxious.

"How far do you think we should go, Widgie?"

"Oh, as far as we can even if we have to swim. The deeper it gets the better barrier it makes against the others."

"Sshh." It was Jen, again, who had heard something.

"What?" whispered Widgie, hardly daring to move.

"Dunno," breathed Jen. "Thought I heard something further up."

They waited and listened, staring ahead into the blackness.

Something metallic was thrown down and it sounded quite near.

"Well, I votes we go down it," said a voice.

Where was it? It came from in front, but how far?

"Orders was we just stand guard this end."

"Ay, but we'll save time if half goes down it and t'other half guards it."

"If orders is we stands guard, we stands guard. Let them Canallers t'other end go down it if they wants to."

"He's right, Gudgeon. It's Bloggs' orders and Bloggs knows what's what."

"How far ahead d'you think they are?" whispered Widgie.

"Only a few hundred feet. We can't seem to go *anywhere* without them blocking us up."

"We'd better go back the way we came. If Jumper and his lot are further up the line now maybe we can creep back to the Bridge."

"If no more engines come," whispered Jen, miserably.

They began to splash their way back, but they'd only gone a couple of steps when a harsh voice echoed through the tunnel from the main line.

"Fools' errand, this." It was Jumper's voice, thought Widgie.

"Jumper's right. You should've let us cover it first time, like I said, Blister."

"Come on anyway—let's get it over with."

There was a moment's silence, and then they heard feet tramping up the tunnel towards them.

"That's it," whispered Jen despairingly. "We've had it. Let's just make sure we stick together when they catch us this time."

The tramping feet got louder, and then they saw a dim yellow light reflected off the walls.

"Don't move," breathed Widgie, and they both nearly jumped out of their skins as a sudden shout echoed right through the tunnel, still from the main line but farther back.

"JUMPER? IS JUMPER THERE?"

"Ay—?" the tramping feet stopped.

"You're to come back. Cap'n's orders. We're all on the move. Rats have taken the Arches. Everyone to report to Camden Lock. Tell them Primrosers to stay guard, Bloggs says. All clear?"

"Ay"—it was Jumper shouting back. Then they heard him say in his normal voice, "Orders 'ere, orders there, too many bloomin' orders."

"Better'n being caught by them Rats," said a voice. "Give 'em a shout t'other end, Jumper."

"Won't hear us from 'ere. Better go further down."

"Bet they will. Anyway you'll get a wetting if you go in further. I know this 'ere tunnel."

There was a moment's silence and then they heard Jumper give a huge bellow.

"Primrose Line?"

"Ay," came an answering shout from the other end. ("Told you they would," said the voice.)

"Bloggs says stay on guard."

"Ay."

"If you gets 'em, go back to Camden. Rats have taken Arches. Clear?"

"Ay; clear enough."

"Come on," said Jumper to his men. "Let's get back before them Rats gets *us*."

The yellow light got dimmer and dimmer until it disappeared and the footsteps gradually receded until they could be heard no more.

Widgie and Jen looked at each other and gave a big sigh of relief—they had been holding their breath most of the time—and then they waded through to the far side of the lake and sat down with their backs against the wall to get over the excitement and to have a think as to what to do next. Jen suppressed a sneeze.

"I've caught a cold, I think," she whispered. "All that

standing in cold water. What shall we do now? Shall we just wait for the Primrosers to go away?"

"Might be a long wait. They all seem to do what they're told, and if they're told to stay on guard—"

"We shouldn't go back to the main tunnel, though. If they're all on the move, or whatever he said, it'll be like Oxford Street on a Saturday. And then if those Rats come after them—"

"Then we'll *have* to wait till they go."

They were both silent for a while, and then Widgie said, "I wonder if I could hurry 'em up a bit."

"Hurry them up?"

"No, I s'pose I couldn't really."

"What *do* you mean, Widgie?"

"Well, they didn't actually *see* Jumper did they? I mean they did what he told them, but they didn't see him."

"No, they didn't *see* him," said Jen patiently.

"I don't expect I could do it, could I, Jen? I mean my voice isn't deep enough."

Light suddenly dawned.

"Oh yes—that's brilliant. I'm *sure* you could."

"They talk rather like people in Dickens, don't they?"

"That's right, of course they do. Do let's try it Widgie. It's worth a *try*. But we'd have to get nearer to them so that only they can hear you."

Widgie started thinking again, and began clearing his throat softly, as if he was experimenting with the lower reaches of his voice.

"O.K. Let's give it a go."

They got up and after a cautious look backwards to make sure there were no unexpected yellow lights left, they began creeping very softly towards the far end of the tunnel. After a little while they stopped and listened carefully. Ahead of them, they could just hear a confused murmur of people chatting in an idle sort of way.

"Go on, Widgie. If it fails we'll just rush back and

take our chance."

Widgie drew a deep breath and concentrated on making his voice low and harsh.

"Primrose Line?" he shouted as loud as he could.

"Ay?"

"Rats be coming. Get back to Camden."

"Rats?"

"Ay. From Arches."

"What about engine?"

"Leave engine, Bloggs said."

"Ay."

"All clear?"

"Ay—clear enough."

"If Rats be coming, we'd best move," said a startled voice.

"Ay, and fast. I ain't seen 'em, but Fudge said they was 'uge."

"I votes we go through tunnel and join t'others. Safety in numbers."

"No blooming fear. That's the way Rats be coming."

"What's Bloggs want with our engine?"

"Dunno. Maybe to take up wounded."

"Well, orders is orders. Can't say I'll be sorry to get back."

There was a confused noise of general movement and of weapons being picked up.

"'Urry up, Gummidge. Don't hang about."

"It's me boots. I took 'em off."

"You won't need yer boots if them Rats gets you. Come on."

The voices got a little fainter as the footsteps retreated and finally there was silence.

"You did it," whispered Jen excitedly.

"Ay," said Widgie, smirking to himself. "Reckon I did."

"Why did you tell them that about the engine?"

"Well they asked me, didn't they? I had to say something."

"Only that now it's there for someone else to chase us with if they want to."

"I didn't think of that," said Widgie, crestfallen.

"Never mind—you did splendidly."

They crept forward cautiously until they could see a dim light at the end of the tunnel, and then they kept close to the wall as a double precaution. When they got near the end, Widgie went first, edging himself forward an inch at a time until he was right next to the entrance.

He squinted round the edge of the tunnel to see if it was all clear, and then beckoned for Jen to join him.

"I think it's alright," he whispered, and they both ventured nervously outside.

"Golly—it's a bit exposed, isn't it," muttered Widgie uneasily.

They were in a very large, airy tunnel. The sides were beautifully made of brick and it had a high arched ceiling above. A double railway track ran down the middle, and there were several sidings on the far side, each ending in a pair of sturdy buffers. A little to their left was an old tank engine, gently smoking. It was painted dark green—an 0-4-2 thought Widgie, interested—and along the side of the water-tank in black letters it said PRIMROSE HILL LINE.

"Yes it is," agreed Jen. "And I can't see any side-tunnels to hide in either. We'll just have to creep along the sides as fast as we can. But which way?"

"Well, all the men on the other line were going up the track to our right, so I s'pose that's the way to Camden. In which case we should go left."

"No—that leads back to Beasley's."

"I don't think it does on this line, otherwise they'd be coming this way as well and they don't seem to be. But I *am* worried about it all being so open and light—look at those ventilation shafts. I can see them from here."

Jen looked up and around.

"If we can't hide, we might as well just run as fast as we

can and cover the ground," she said.

"Shall we do that, then?" she said again when he didn't answer.

She looked at him and saw him lost in thought.

"*Widgie*," she said impatiently.

"It can't be *so* difficult," he said to himself.

"What *are* you talking about?"

"I suppose I could try."

"Try *what*?"

"But supposing it blew up. That's always a risk."

"Oh, you're impossible."

"But I did watch Bloggs quite carefully."

"Widgie—are we going to run or not?"

"Wait a minute."

He looked carefully up and down the track, and then he nipped smartly across to the engine and climbed into the cab. Jen watched, open-mouthed.

Widgie sat down on the little round driver's seat and thought.

He thought about Bloggs when he had been in the cab with him and when he had been peering round the tender from the first truck. Then he looked at the controls, and went through everything he could remember, in mime, without touching anything.

The trouble was that nothing was labelled with neat metal plates like they were on the *Flying Blogger*, so he had to try to remember which was which.

"That's the Regulator, I know," he said to himself. "And that's the Steam Brake, and this is the Valve Gear, I think. I can't read all those gauges even if I could remember what they are, so they'll have to take care of themselves. I think it's that Regulator that's most important; at any rate, to start with."

He looked at them all again and thought deeply.

"I'm going to have a go," he called out. "Nip across quickly."

"Do you think you can?" she said breathlessly, as she climbed up beside him.

"We'll soon find out, won't we?" He grinned. "You'll have to keep the fire stoked."

"Of course," said Jen impatiently. "Here's the shovel," and she promptly burned her fingers opening the fire-box. She peered in.

"It's awfully hot, and burning like anything—I'll only have to keep it going."

"You'll have to do more than that," said Widgie. "You'll have to build it up till the top part's really molten. And there's something about when you leave the fire-door open and when you shut it."

"Well, I think it'll be open most of the time because of building it up. Shall we go, Widgie?"

"Are you ready, Stoker?"

"Ay, Driver," said Jen, shovelling in the first shovelful.

Widgie, feeling more than a little nervous, opened the regulator and heard the chimney begin to bark as the exhaust steam and smoke puffed out of it. Then he put the Reversing Gear to forwards as he remembered Bloggs doing it, and the wheels began to turn slowly and *Chuff* went the tanker—*Chuff, chuff*, as the pistons rotated faster. Widgie opened the regulator still more, and the engine began to gather speed—"Bravo, driver," shouted Jen, shovelling like mad.

Hotter and hotter grew the fire, quicker and quicker came the *chuffs*, faster and faster the *clickety-clacks* as the wheels jolted over the rails. Widgie was exhilarated and terrified at the same time, because although he seemed to have managed to start, he wasn't at all sure whether he could do anything else. He and Jen were soon sweating with heat from the firebox and Widgie suddenly realized that neither of them had looked up to see where they were going —Jen because of the shovelling and he because he had been trying to understand all his gauges and dials.

He peered ahead through the driver's window but he couldn't see anything because the whole engine seemed to be enveloped in a blanket of steam; I hope Jumper hasn't mucked up the tracks down here as well, he thought. He leant out of the cab as far as he dared, to avoid the steam, and managed to see a little.

"There are points ahead," he shouted to Jen. "The tunnel's dividing—I've no idea where we're going."

"Never mind," shouted Jen, caught up in the excitement of the moment. "Anywhere, driver."

Widgie took the points too fast, and the engine gave a great lurch, sparks flew everywhere and, with an enormous clattering from the rails, it swung to the left, into the smaller tunnel. The noise was quite frightening and Widgie half-shut the regulator in the hope that the tanker would slow down.

"We're onto single track now."

"What happens if one comes the other way?" shouted Jen, resting a moment.

"We jump. Hey—look out. Duck out of sight, there's a station coming up."

Widgie flattened himself against the controls so that he couldn't be seen, and Jen crouched down with the coals in the coal-bunker. The two platforms leapt towards them and, as Widgie peered through the cab-windows, he saw groups of Railwaymen staring and waving in what seemed to be a panic-stricken way. He tried to read the name of the station but the signs flashed by too quickly, and in a moment it was left behind.

"All clear," he shouted, and Jen got to her feet and started shovelling again.

"Where was it, Widgie?"

"I don't know; couldn't see. But they were all waving in a funny way."

"Maybe we're on a dead-end line or something. D'you

know how to stop it?"

"I'm not sure—it was as much as I could do to start it."

In fact, Widgie's mind had been occupied solely with the problems of slowing up and stopping ever since he had started, and he had been eyeing something that he thought might be the Brake Handle speculatively for some time. He glanced up the line and noted with satisfaction that they were on a straight stretch—no worries for the moment.

"Widgie—what's that light? It's coming towards us I think."

Widgie looked again and his heart sank. It was an engine, in the distance admittedly, but fast approaching. Widgie groaned to himself. It was a single track, and if he managed to stop, which he didn't think he could, they would have to confront, and probably be recaptured by, the Railwaymen in the oncoming engine; if he drove straight ahead a head-on collision was inevitable.

There was another shout from Jen: "There's a passing place on my side, Widgie," and suddenly a plan, or the outline of one, flashed across Widgie's mind.

"Jen—see that cord above your head? That's the whistle. Grab hold of it and hang on for all you're worth."

An ear-splitting blast, never-ending, echoed down the tunnel as Widgie rummaged in the locker by the coal-bunker. "Ah, *that's* it," he said to himself, and chucked a green flag at Jen. "Wave that so they can see it, but keep the whistle going."

He rushed back to his controls, sent up a quick prayer, shut his eyes, and turned what he thought might be the Brake Handle to the left. There was a gush of steam and the tanker began slowing down a little. Widgie gave a sigh of relief and watched the effect of all this on the approaching engine.

It was dramatic. The engine stopped in a cloud of smoke through which the fireman could occasionally be seen waving a red flag. The driver himself dashed to the passing place points and switched them over, then ran back and raised steam again, and finally the engine jerked forward and left the line clear, as it shunted into the passing place.

Not a moment too soon, thought Widgie, who had been trying unsuccessfully to slow the tanker down even more, in order to give them time to accomplish this manoeuvre. Jen was still hanging on to the whistle and waving a frenzied green flag when Widgie suddenly realized the fatal flaw in his plan.

"The points are wrong," he said to himself in an agony of realization.

He wasn't even going to try to stop, only to get themselves both recaptured, so he did exactly the opposite in the wild hope that he could crash the points over. He turned off the Brake Handle and moved the Reversing Gear up to 15 degrees. He felt the tanker surge forwards, and he looked down the line to see how much distance he had to get up speed. Only about half-a-mile.

"Hold tight, Jen. If we crash, jump and then follow me."

Jen abandoned her flag and whistle and they both wedged themselves into corners and held on. The tanker took the points at about forty miles an hour. It had no bogies so it was the big driving wheels which took the impact. For a split second they were suspended in mid-air, then the right-hand wheel-flange caught the right-hand rail of the points, and in a moment of terrifying impact it forced the points over, and with a great lurch to the left it settled back onto the tracks.

Widgie looked to see if Jen was alright—she was white with shock—and then back at the other engine. The two Railwaymen were staring at the retreating tanker in fury and amazement, and Widgie realized that they had been spotted and that chase would be given as soon as they could re-set the points and raise steam.

"We'll have to get rid of the engine soon, Jen. They saw me."

Jen nodded and took a look up the line before going back to her shovelling. "Duck, Widgie," she shouted. "Station coming up."

Widgie flattened himself up against the controls again and looked through the right-hand cab window. There was only one platform this time and it was packed tight with Railwaymen, all holding their pickaxes and shovels and talking to themselves.

They're almost bound to see us, thought Widgie, Oh, well, I suppose it doesn't matter much now.

He tried to read the name of the station again, and this time he managed it. LISSON GROVE, it said, and as the tanker roared by he caught a glimpse of startled faces and people pointing at it.

"Jen," he shouted.

"Yes?"

"After the next points I'll try to stop and we'll run for it. O.K.?"

"O.K."

"Give us more steam, then. We need as much distance between us and them as we can get."

Dig, swing, throw; dig, swing, throw, thought Jen to herself as she built up the fire.

Widgie could see a good straight stretch of line ahead, so he opened the regulator and watched the track. He could see *something* in front of them—what was it? Yes—just what he needed—the tunnel was dividing at a set of points.

Which way shall we be taken I wonder?

Out loud he said, "You can stop shovelling now, but hold tight."

He watched the track division looming nearer and nearer and tried to figure out which way they would turn by concentrating on the points, but steam from the chimney was floating downwards and getting in his way. At last they hit them with a jolt and the tanker swung to the left.

At the first bend, he thought, I'll pull and push *everything* and hope for the best.

The bend was almost immediately upon them, and Widgie hurled himself at everything—the blower, the regulator, the brakes and anything else he could find. A rush of steam enveloped the whole engine and there was a strong smell rather like garlic as the tanker ground to an inelegant halt.

"Stay there," shouted Widgie. He jumped down from the cab and ran as hard as he could back round the bend to the points. They were heavy but well-oiled, and the lever responded clumsily but certainly as he pulled it back. The points slid across, but before Widgie could run back he saw the engine coming into the long straight stretch.

"Where to hide?" he asked himself, panic-stricken. There was nowhere, so he stretched himself out flat behind the points and hoped for the best.

As the engine got nearer he could see that it *was* the one he had forced into the passing-place, but now it was crowded with as many Railwaymen as it would hold.

They must have picked them up at the station, thought Widgie, with dismay. Luckily the engine was travelling in reverse, so its visibility was limited. Widgie tucked his head down and put his hands over it as the engine rushed by and took the right fork. Once it was out of sight, he scrambled to his feet and ran back to Jen.

"Come on, Jen—more running," he said as he dragged her out of the cab, her face so covered with soot and coal-dust that he had to laugh.

"You should see yours," retorted Jen. "What did you do?"

"Changed the points so that it took the other line," said Widgie proudly.

"I wonder how long it'll take them to find out."

"When they get to the next station, for sure."

"So we ought to have ten minutes start."

"If we're lucky. Come on, Jen."

They set off up the track, trotting so as to save their

breath, and both of them felt a sense of false safety and security after their mad and dangerous journey in the tanker.

"We don't know *where* we're running to," said Jen, beginning to puff.

"If we can just lose ourselves, so that they don't know *where* we are, we'll have time to think out a plan," said Widgie. "That's what I'm hoping for anyway."

Jen saved her breath, although what she was thinking was that she wished they could find a canal with a boat, because they seemed to have so many more side-tunnels than the railway tunnels did. The tunnel they were in now, for instance, although quite light and airy, had no turn-offs at all that she could see, and they must have been running for at least ten minutes. Suddenly there was a familiar sound, and she stopped in mid-stride.

Chuff, chuff; chuff, they heard behind them, although quite a long way behind them.

"Come on," panted Widgie, and they both put on their best turn of speed.

"They must have started up our tanker," said Jen.

"I know. I'd hoped it was bust after the way I stopped it."

"We need a plan, Widgie, it'll be on top of us in a moment."

Widgie was trying to think of one but he couldn't because of the running. They were both absolutely flat out now, arms and legs flying like pistons, and all the time the chuffing and clanking got louder behind them.

"Can't do much more," panted Jen.

"Keep going till the next bend."

They got to it, and round it, and both stopped in a flurry of amazement and indecision. They had joined a new tunnel that came right across them—another big one with double-tracks and sidings, and with a high roof.

"Quick, double back!"—and they both shot down it to the right and almost at once saw a truck with tarpaulin over it standing in a tiny siding. "Dodge behind here," gasped Widgie, feeling as if his heart would burst in a minute. They just made it, as their old tanker lurched out into the big tunnel and carried along it to the left, the Railwaymen in the cab and on top of the coal-bunker, looking eagerly in all directions.

"They've missed us," said Jen excitedly, as they watched the tanker disappearing up the track.

"Keep your head down. They're still looking." Widgie was peering all round the new tunnel to see if it held any new opportunities for them. He was deeply distrustful of these big main lines, and preferred the smaller, darker tunnels where there was less risk of being taken by surprise.

"What's that over there?" He pointed to the opposite wall.

"Can't see a thing."

"Come over here. Look, between those two trucks in that siding."

"Oh, I see. Yes—I think you're right. It's not a tunnel, it's a sort of very large drain. Let's go and look—quick."

They were just going to dash across the tracks when Widgie stopped, cocked an ear, and pulled her back.

"Why?" said Jen, surprised.

"Something's coming from up the line. Another train, I think."

They crouched down once more and, sure enough, about a minute later an engine appeared behind them, travelling fast in the same direction as the tanker. But not just an engine—coupled up behind were five or six passenger coaches and they were filled to the brim with Railwaymen armed with picks and shovels.

"Look at that," said Jen, as they watched it pass. "They're really bringing up the reinforcements."

They waited a moment until it had disappeared, following the tanker, and then, with an extra cautious look all round, they both ran across to the other side of the tunnel, hid behind the two trucks for a moment, and then crept over to examine the 'drain'.

It was about two feet off the ground, the entrance neatly framed with bricks, and it ran steeply up-hill, into the wall as it were. But in spite of looking a bit drain-like it was actually quite large—perhaps six feet in diameter, and although unfinished insofar as the floor and sides were of rock or sand, it had oil lamps hung from the walls at intervals of about twenty feet. Widgie and Jen were delighted with it.

"That's for us," said Widgie. "It looks as if it goes somewhere, it's well-lit and it goes uphill which is what we want."

"It's the well-lit bit I don't like," said Jen. "They must use it a good deal. Hey, look out, Widgie—our tanker's coming back, and so's the other one. That settles it," and she climbed into the drain followed as quickly as he could by Widgie. It was so steep that they had to go on hands and knees, and after they'd climbed in about thirty feet they found a small cavity to their right. They edged themselves into it for a moment so that they could check that the tanker and the train passed safely by, and they looked at each other with dismay, therefore, when they heard the hiss of steam and the clanking of couplings as either one or both—they couldn't tell which—drew up nearby. They heard people jumping onto the track and tramping up and down.

"They must be 'iding somewhere near 'ere," said a voice.

"I'll swear they weren't on the Lisson Grove Link when we came down it and we've both checked out everything for about a mile down track."

"What about up toward Paddington?"

"That's the way we came and they weren't there. No sign, and I had fifty men in our coaches looking, too."

"In that case we've got 'em."

"Right—check all these trucks first, under the tarpaulins and all, and then we'll spread out both ways for five hundred yards and do it proper."

"I want to get our tanker back to depot—they've fair mucked it up. Me inside big end was so hot it'd be no surprise if 'twas cracked."

"Alright, but take it back to Camden, then you can report to Bloggs. Tell 'im they're here somewhere and we've got fifty men looking."

"Don't forget the Dead End up there."

"I won't forget nothing, but I'm covering the track first. If they're up that, they'll keep. Dead End." The voice chuckled. "Tell Bloggs from me, this *is* the Dead End."

17

The Dead End

Widgie and Jen waited a moment until the noise of the tanker getting up steam and of the men lifting tarpaulins and generally tramping around was sufficient to cover their movements, and then they clambered up from the cavity and began climbing their Dead End.

"I don't mind if it *is* a dead end," said Widgie bravely. "We'll go up it, and when we get to the top or wherever it goes, we'll fight 'em tooth and nail. They'll only be able to get one or two abreast in this place."

"Right," said Jen, matching his mood although she didn't feel much like it. "That's the spirit. Anyway, I *like* this drain—well-lit and cosy."

After it had wound round twice—once to the right and once left, it levelled out into a sort of rocky room, half-filled with old picks and shovels, and then narrowed down again and continued climbing even more steeply. The lanterns on the walls became more infrequent and the roof a little lower, but it was still easily big enough for them to walk upright. They had no need to go on hands and knees now, because when the pitch became too steep for comfort someone had carved rough steps into the floor. The only thing that worried them was the air, which was becoming uncomfortably stuffy, partly, no doubt, because of the heat from the lanterns but also because there were no ventilation shafts.

They had been climbing solidly for perhaps five minutes after having left the rocky room, when Widgie, who was in front, stopped and held a finger up for silence. They both listened, and, to their dismay, they heard the unmistakable sound of a train passing—but passing, so it seemed, right by the wall immediately on their right.

"That's odd," said Widgie. "It must be another of their systems *above* the big one below."

"Can't hear it chuffing," said Jen.

"Nor can I. But it's clanking. Anyway, let's get on. I want to get to the end of this before we formulate plans."

The train noise disappeared as they climbed higher, and then the tunnel began behaving most eccentrically—it couldn't seem to decide where to go. It would turn left quite sharply, then equally sharply right, then it would begin to slope downhill—once quite steeply, so that a dozen steps had been cut—and then slope equally steeply uphill, then turn again and again in the same direction so that it was almost a spiral, and then level out and run straight ahead with great determination only to make a turn at the end that appeared to double back in the direction it had just come from.

Widgie and Jen totally lost track of which way they were facing or whether the big main line was behind them or in front of them—the only thing they knew for sure was that it was beneath them, and, indeed, quite a long way beneath them. Finally the tunnel made a determined right turn, went up twenty-four steep steps, turned right again—almost a right angle—and ended.

This was the Dead End—a small room about twelve feet square, yet for some reason nearly twenty feet high and lit by a solitary lantern. They both sat down, partly from exhaustion at climbing so many steps and partly from resignation, because the men had been right again. They'd said it was a dead end and a dead end it was—the deadest of dead ends right in the middle of a lot of rock. It was like a tomb, Jen decided, looking around it; which, she supposed, was appropriate enough because she had gradually been deciding in her mind that there was no way that they could ever escape from this extraordinary world.

As she looked round the room—which was, in an odd and very bare way rather interesting because it definitely *was* a room and not just a cavern—she suddenly became aware that they had automatically sat down not on the floor but on *something*, although they had been too exhausted to notice what.

She looked down at it in a still puffed and idle sort of way, and then jumped up as if she had been stung.

"Widgie—LOOK."

Widgie, who had his head nearly between his knees because he knew that that was the best way to get one's breath back, looked up startled.

"What?"

"Look what we're sitting on. It's a *Bump*. It's like *our* Bump. The one that started it all—we're sitting on it. Well, not the *same* Bump, but it is the same in shape and, yes, it's the same all over. It's a real Bump. Oh dear, but there's no key. And anyway, the Bump led *down* to this place and we're still in it so it can't be leading down to it; how confusing, because if we're still *here* why is there a Bump? I mean—look Widgie, this is important—if there's a Bump here it ought to be in the roof and it ought to be the other side of the Bump that we look at—the hollowed out side with the rope in it, *and* there ought to be a slit and the Down Line Ladder. Why do they want one here at all?"

Widgie had listened to all this with great interest, because he saw precisely what Jen meant. It was definitely odd. But one thing he knew the answer to, and, with a certain modesty and yet with a certain pride, he took off his left boot and turned it upside down.

Something tinkled onto the floor.

"What is it, Widgie?" Jen bent down and picked it up. "It's a key! Where did you find it?"

"I just kept it. I thought it might be useful later," said

Widgie, smirking as he had after his imitation of the Railway voice, but Jen was already on her hands and knees, muttering to herself.

"Wait a minute—the bolt was fairly low down. I can't tell which side it was, of course, but I think it was—there! Widgie, look. I've found it—*just* like the other one."

She put the key in and fiddled it one way and then the other and at last she got the position right and she turned it right round full circle.

There was a metallic creaking noise, and very slowly indeed the Bump began to open like a hatch being pushed up from inside. It really made very little noise, but when it was standing upright like an open lid, it gave a small sigh like a compressed air door opening and it gently flopped back onto the floor.

They crept forward, peering down together.

"Oh no," cried Jen in despair, although what else she had expected to find after her previous thoughts she couldn't have said.

They were looking down through a fairly large iron grille onto just another part of the system, and as they looked, a train rumbled by.

"I can't bear it," moaned Jen. "I thought it must lead *somewhere*."

But there were the same little tracks and the same little tunnels—not, however the same trains. True, it was little—in fact considerably smaller than the ones they were used to— but instead of ordinary trucks and coaches, these trucks were more like long metal platforms, and they were loaded with metal containers with canvas tops that came to a peak at the top like small tents.

They watched a little longer and another one rattled by, going the opposite way.

"It's a double track," said Widgie. "It must be their system for transporting food and things."

"If it's food, let's jump down and have some. I've

never been so hungry in my life."

They waited only a minute, watching, and then another one went in the same direction as the first.

"They don't have proper engines," said Widgie in an interested voice. "At least not steam engines. How do they run?"

"Oh, don't get all mechanical—*I* thought we were going to get out."

"Well, I knew we wouldn't get *out*, because it leads downwards, and out is upwards, but the main thing is that it gets us out of this dead end. At least I hope it does. Is there a rope ladder inside the Bump?"

"Not even that," said Jen, groping around inside it.

"We'll have to jump then. Let's get this iron grille off."

Widgie knelt down and curled his fingers through the bars.

"Here we go," he said, and gave a huge pull. Nothing happened.

"Listen, Jen—while I'm doing this, have a look inside the Bump. I'm sure there must be a keyhole there for closing it. Probably opposite the outside one."

"We don't need to *close* it, surely? Let's just get through."

Widgie was still struggling with the grille heaving it and pushing it in all directions.

"We *do* need to," he panted. "Then they won't know where we've gone."

"Alright, I'll find it. And, by the way, I bet that's got a catch underneath it—probably one each side—and then it just drops onto the line."

Widgie looked at her silently and felt underneath it, and there, sure enough, were two iron catches. He began pushing at them. Then he pulled the grille upwards at the same time, to lessen the weight on the catches, and he managed to shove one aside. The grille lurched downwards on one side and Widgie did the same on the other. With a heavy crash, the grille fell down onto the tracks right in the path of an oncoming train.

"Oh gosh," said Widgie in dismay. "They're bound to have seen that."

"They might not," said Jen, searching the inside of the Bump. "Or they'll think it's just an accident. Hey—I've found it! You were right—it's opposite the bolt on the outside. Wait a minute." She got the key out of the bolt and tried to fit it on the inside. "Yes, it fits, Widgie. How's that?"

They both looked at it with satisfaction and shook hands.

"All we've got to do now is to jump through."

"Well, its about twelve feet and those trains are fairly frequent. I think it's too risky Widgie. But I tell you what—"

"If we jump *onto* a train—"

"Those canvas tops will soften the fall and we shan't risk being run over."

"And we shan't have to jump so far."

"It'll want careful timing," said Jen thoughtfully. "Particularly if we close the Bump after us."

"But the trains don't seem to go very fast—here's another. Let's watch."

They both watched it go by with a professional eye.

"Some of the containers are empty, with no canvas. They might be better, but they'd hurt more."

"Let's try for them," said Jen. "Then we can hide inside them. But we can only drop on the ones going to the right. Does that matter?"

"I don't think it matters which way we go," said Widgie, "Because we'll have to jump off fairly soon anyway. Left is towards Beasley's and right is towards Camden, I suppose, although I rather lost sense of direction on the way up here."

"So did I. Well, we'd better not hang around, because they'll be sending someone up here to look for us soon. They said they would."

As if in answer to Jen's fears, they heard distant voices down the tunnel.

"That settles it," whispered Widgie. "The next one, then."

He got his fingers on the key in readiness and from the left below, they heard the now familiar rumble and rattle.

"You first, Jen."

"It's coming," said Jen peering down, "I can just see the engine."

"I'm turning the key, Jen. Jump as soon as you see the trucks."

To his joy he saw the Bump slowly beginning to close.

"Quick," he said urgently.

"Here they are ... I'm jumping—"

Her last word was lost in a scream as she disappeared.

The Bump was standing upright now and Widgie could hear the mens' voices behind him quite clearly, so he shut his eyes, folded his arms over his chest and jumped. His stomach turned over as he felt himself fall, and then he hit the canvas top of a full container with a thud, half missing it and banging his knees on the metal edges.

"Ow," he shouted, not minding who heard, and he grabbed the sides to stop himself falling onto the track. He looked backwards, and upwards immediately and he thought he saw the Bump safely shut, but he couldn't be sure. He waited a moment to get his breath back and then took stock of his situation. As far as he could see the train had only two long trucks with three containers in each, and he was in the very last. Thank goodness, he thought. I nearly missed it altogether.

He peered forward but it was so dark that he could see almost nothing. "Jen?" he shouted, as he clung to the lurching truck. "Jen?"

There was no answer, so he began edging forwards, pulling himself along with his hands on the edges of the containers. The first one was empty, so he climbed into it and felt a bit more comfortable.

"Jen?" Still no answer. Had she missed the trucks altogether as he nearly had? Perhaps she was still lying on the track underneath the Bump. He climbed out of the empty container and negotiated the gap between the two trucks—it was quite a small gap luckily—and got on top of the last container of the first truck. Still no sign.

"Jen?" he shouted as loudly as he could, not even minding if the driver heard him.

"Here Widgie."

"Thank goodness"—he could just see her hand waving cautiously at him from right up front. He climbed forward to her and found her crouching down in the very first container, an empty one.

"Done it," he breathed, sliding down next to her and feeling himself all over.

"Did the Bump shut alright?" asked Jen.

"I think so—at any rate I only got out just in time."

"The tops are quite soft aren't they? It *must* be food."

"Not for me they weren't—I hit the edge."

"Ow . . . you must be bruised all over."

"A bit, I think."

They peered over the top and looked around them. The tunnel was a small one, perhaps only ten feet in diameter and very dark, and the engine, which was right in front of them, had no coal-tender and seemed totally enclosed, so they couldn't see the driver.

Jen looked backwards. "I'm going to open that canvas thing and see if it's food. I'm starving."

"Better not, Jen—we may come to a station any minute, and then we'll have to jump off and hide. Let's hope there's only one platform, then we can get off on the opposite side and double back without being seen."

"Oh dear, I'm so tired of escaping all the time."

"So am I; but this time we'll have time to rest somewhere, because they won't know *where* we are now."

There was a roaring noise as a train approached from the other direction, and they both ducked their heads down so as not to be seen. Their train gave a lurch as the track curved round sharply to the right, and they clung on to the sides to keep their balance, at the same time taking the opportunity to have a look ahead.

"I can see lights," said Jen, as the curve straightened out, "But a long way off."

"So can I. I think it's a station. Get ready to hide if it goes straight through and to jump off if it stops. If we jump, double up as low as you can and follow me. I shall go backwards behind the trucks."

Jen leant further over her side and she could just see a long platform, very brightly lit.

"It *is* a station, and the platform's on my side. That means we jump off on yours."

The train began to slow down slightly.

"It *is* going to stop, Jen; we'd better jump long before the station otherwise we'll be seen. I don't know what we do if a train comes on the other track. Anyway, tell me when we're about thirty feet away." He was calculating the speed of the train against the rails and trying to decide how long it would take them to clamber over the sides.

Jen peered out cautiously. "About a hundred yards to go, Widgie. Seventy. Fifty. Better do it now rather than too late. We're nearly there... it's a very *bright* station. THIRTY FEET......HEY, STOP....HOLD IT ... DON'T JUMP....IT'S GOT...WHY IT'S GOT...*STOP*. WIDGIE ...LOOK!"

The train drew up smoothly at the station.

"Blimey, Bert," said a voice. "Look what they've sent with the mail today."

With a clatter, their container was slid off the truck and onto the platform.

Widgie and Jen looked up, and Bert and the voice looked down, and for a moment they all regarded each other in silence.

Then Widgie looked round and saw a sign with a red light under it that said, SHUNT, CAR SHED, STOP. Next to it another sign said, WESTBOUND.

"What 'ave you two been up to then?" said Bert.

Widgie and Jen looked at each other.

Bert rubbed his nose. "I think we'd better get the Inspector down—I don't know 'ow to 'andle this one."

Widgie and Jen climbed awkwardly out of their container onto the platform and began to take in their surroundings. They were on a long platform in quite a high, well-lit tunnel and there were lots more containers on it and they were being handled by real grown-up men.

Real grown-up men.

It was all lit by electric light as well.

Widgie and Jen were past speech—they just stood and stared.

In a moment Bert returned with the Inspector, who was wearing a peaked cap.

"My goodness, you two look in a fair mess. What are *you* doing on the Post Office Railway?"

Jen looked at Widgie and Widgie looked at Jen, and then they both looked up at the Inspector.

"I suppose you know you're trespassing," he said. "It's an offence to ride with Her Majesty's Mail."

"We were only having a look," said Widgie helplessly.

"We've always been interested," said Jen.

"But how did you *get* on it?" asked the Inspector, really wanting to know.

"It was—er—sort of further up the line," said Widgie vaguely.

Light suddenly dawned on Bert's face.

"*I* know what it is. They're from one of them School Parties brought down to see the Railway. Must have 'idden from the rest and stayed down."

"Is *that* it?" said the Inspector, somewhat relieved.

"Well, sort of," said Jen.

"Where d'you live?"

"Two hundred and eighty-four Cranley Gardens, Muswell Hill," said Jen eagerly, "and we'd very much like to get back there, please, if you'll let us off this time."

The Inspector took off his cap and scratched his head.

"The Crouch End van's leaving in ten minutes," said Bert, summing up the situation. "I s'pose they could drop 'em off. They look a bit messy for Public Transport."

"Irregular," said the Inspector, still scratching.

"Oh, *please*," said Widgie and Jen, almost together.

"I'll take 'em up," said Bert, "And tell 'em not to do it again."

* * *

And that was how Widgie and Jen came to be delivered home with the morning mail.

Their parents had been up all night—Mum mostly crying and Dad making useless cups of tea.

"But where have you *been*?" asked Mum, still crying but in a different way.

"You'd better leave this to me, dear," said Dad, furious with relief. "But first of all, you two should go up and have a bath and get out of those clothes and get some iodine and sticking-plaster on yourselves."

"What can we *say*?" asked Jen hopelessly as they both tried to patch each other up in the bathroom. "We *can't* tell the truth. It would just be too impossible, and one thing would lead to another and there would never be any end to it."

"I think Bert had the right idea," said Widgie. "We just joined up with these kids who were being shown round the Post Office whatever-it-is, and you and I got lost and had to stay down the whole night, and that's how we got into this state trying to find a way out. After all, it's partly true—it is a *sort* of secret railway."

So they tried it on, and no matter how hard Dad looked at them, they stuck to it; and really, all four of them were so glad to be together again that in the end that was all that mattered.

"Anyway, next time you'd better stick to the Underground," said Dad.

Widgie and Jen looked at each other and grinned.

"O.K., Dad," they said.

APPENDIX A:

The End of the Story

The complete history of Widgie and Jen's discovery of the North London system is written up in the Records, but here it is proposed to reproduce the latter stages only, from the point at which the Railwaymen finally lost contact with them at Dead End. This was on the main Paddington—Kings Cross line at the point where it is met by the Lisson Grove Link and it will be no surprise to those who have read the whole story to learn that the search begun there failed to find any trace of them. What is perhaps of more interest is that the detachment sent to investigate the Dead End found the Observation Shaft—referred to by Widgie and Jen as the Bump—safely shut and in good order.

We know that the trainload of Railwaymen who nearly caught Widgie and Jen dashing out from behind the truck, came from Paddington, having been despatched there by the Tanker Driver when he realized that they must have taken the Lisson Grove Link after all.

The driver of the Paddington Train was a highly-respected Railwayman named Jugger, and when he reported back to Bloggs at Camden Lock that he had found no trace of the Abovegrounders there was a long silence. Not having been there, it was difficult for Bloggs to in any way criticize Jugger's methods of conducting the search, yet the news of his failure, coming so soon after his optimistic message, "This *is* the Dead End", could not but cause concern. So much so that Bloggs called an immediate meeting of the whole search party which was—an unusual occurrence, this—

reported verbatim in the Records, Bloggs obviously assuming the role of a Prosecuting Counsel.

Part of this enquiry is here reproduced:

Bloggs: Blagfast [the name of the Tanker Driver]—you says you first spotted the Abovegrounders when you was forced into the passing place 'twixt Grand Union and Lisson Grove?

Blagfast: Ay.

Bloggs: No mistakes? By which I mean, be you sure?

Blagfast: Ay. First, I sees 'em, second, who else would steam straight ahead when 'e sees an oncoming engine on a single track? Not a Railwayman.

Bloggs: And thus you followed?

Blagfast: Ay.

Bloggs: 'Ow long, Blagfast, 'twixt spotting 'em and following 'em?

Blagfast: Give it they had three minutes start by the time I changed points and got up steam again.

Bloggs: CHANGED POINTS? You means they got out and changed points and you didn't catch 'em?

Blagfast: They drives straight through 'em. Points was set against 'em but they puts on steam and forces 'em over. 'Twas a 0-4-2. No bogies.

Bloggs: Danged Widgie-boy. Was they bent?

Blagfast: Ay, a bit.

Bloggs: So then you gives chase?

Blagfast: Ay. Picked up some men at Lisson Grove first.

Bloggs: And you goes on to Paddington?

Blagfast: Ay. If they couldn't stop against an oncoming on a single track I figgers they went the way the points took 'em at the Lisson Grove Link, and they was set for Paddington.

Bloggs: And was you right?

Blagfast: No, I was wrong, 'cos when I draws in at Paddington, no-one's seen sight nor heard sound of 'em.

Bloggs: So not to put too fine a point on it, you realizes you've been caught napping?

Blagfast: I realize they 'ave gone down the Link after all, Bloggs, if that's what ye mean. There weren't no other possibility; so I calls on Jugger here to take a train-load down the main King's Cross line to cut 'em off while I goes back to the Link.

Bloggs: And what does you find in Link, Blagfast?

Blagfast: I finds their tanker—'twas a Camden lock tanker —abandoned just round first bend. Nearly hits it, I does. I can't get past it, so we transfers to it and tries to get the danged thing going. Terrible state she were in—big-end nearly burnt out and wheels out of true—but we manages it and proceeds onward to join up with Jugger's lot.

Bloggs: So when you gets to main Paddington—King's Cross line, Blagfast, does you assume them two would double back towards Paddington?

Blagfast: If they doubles back I makes the assumption that Jugger gets 'em, and thus I proceed onward to King's Cross to deal with t'other eventuality.

Bloggs: And there they wasn't?

Blagfast: Not a sign.

Bloggs: But 'ere we're dealing with double track, sidings and all. How was it, Blagfast, you was so sure?

Blagfast: Beggin' ye pardon, Bloggs, I wasn't sure; but speed was, as is said, of an essence, and I considered it me dooty to cover the ground.

Bloggs: So how far up the line does you go, Blagfast?

Blagfast: I goes no more'n a mile, 'cos I figgers them Abovegrounders can't get further no matter 'ow hard they runs. Then I reverses back to give it another going over, and then I meets Jugger with 'is train-load, so we stops and 'as a parley and we agrees that I takes the old tanker back to Camden and Jugger starts the search

	where Link joins Main. At which point, in accordance with Rules, I hands over command to Jugger seeing as he's commanding more men.
Bloggs:	Right and proper. So now Jugger it is me dooty to ask you what proceeded.
Jugger:	We backs down to the junction 'twixt Main and Link, Bloggs, as you would yeself, and we conducts a search. Close on fifty men I 'ad with me and we looks everywhere, up Link as well.
Bloggs:	Looks in all trucks, lifts tarpaulins?
Jugger:	What d'ye take me for, Bloggs—a fool? Ay.
Bloggs:	'Ow far up line?
Jugger:	We searches fast on a mile either way.
Bloggs:	Dead End?
Jugger:	Ay, five men went up Dead End.
Bloggs:	When?
Jugger:	Not ten minutes after we starts looking.
Bloggs:	There be an Observation Shaft up Dead End if me memory serves me right, put in to hobserve this 'ere new power system.
Jugger:	All shut and sealed up proper.
Bloggs:	Who went up?
Voice:	Me—I went up with Grabber and Slanter and Bolger and someone else—who was it?
Voice:	Me—Budger.
Voice:	That's right—Budger it was.
Bloggs:	Who be that that speaks?
Voice:	I be Puddle.
Bloggs:	What d'ye find, Puddle?
Puddle:	Nought. All in place.
Bloggs:	Footprints?
Puddle:	Don't find no footprints up Dead End, Bloggs. It's all rock. But you take me word, there weren't no-one there, and the Shaft were proper shut and locked.

Bloggs: Right. Now, Jugger, it's for you to describe the search and it's for me to find the gaps. I doesn't like doing it, but it's us that lost 'em, and the Cap'n 'ere is listening to every word we utter and I don't blame 'im. We be what's called responsible. Now we'll begin at the moment you starts searching. How many trucks was in the sidings?. . . . .
. . . .

[An hour of detailed questioning, here omitted]

Captain: So it seems, Bloggs, they're lost.

Bloggs: It seems so, Cap'n. We 'ave been what's called outwitted.

Captain: Not *we*, Bloggs. At the point when they was lost it appears to have been a Railway concern.

Bloggs: If so you wish it, Cap'n, the Railway has been outwitted. But now them Abovegrounders has the whole system open to 'em, Canals and Railway alike, I suggests we sink what may be called petty differences and draws up a joint plan of campaign.

Captain: Ay, Bloggs; as long as it's straight in the Records who lost 'em, I agrees; and I further suggests we include in this 'ere plan of campaign our other enemies.

Bloggs: Meaning, Cap'n?

Captain: The Rats, Bloggs. Don't forget 'em.

* * *

It was not unnatural, of course, that the Rats should have been very much to the forefront of the Captain's mind. It was, after all, *his* headquarters that the Rats had taken over, and to have to make a temporary home at Camden Lock was uncomfortable for all the Beasley's Arches' Canallers. Indeed, a study of the Records shows that the Plan of Campaign discussions were partly confused by the

Captain insisting on dealing with the Rats as a first priority and Bloggs equally insisting that, until the Abovegrounders were found, everything else should take second place. Also, emerging from the odd sentence or two, it had become increasingly clear that, lurking at the back of both their minds, was the fact that no-one knew who had really won the Battle and to whom, now, did Beasley's really belong?

In the event, it reflects very much to the credit of both that a workable plan was arrived at to deal, in some measure at least, with all these matters. An extract of the signed agreement produced at the end of the discussions is here reproduced with comments:

1. *It is agreed that the entire North London system be mobilized to search for the Abovegrounders.* [This was no small undertaking, involving as it did the sending of messages to some twenty-five stations and thirteen wharves. In the end, it was accomplished by ordering Primrose Hill to alert the whole Western sector including the Swiss and Holly, and Great North Road to deal with the Grafton-Caledonian central sector. A similar system was adopted by the Canallers, and a later entry in the Records shows that the whole system was involved in the search within three hours].

2. *It is agreed that a Rat Reconnaissance be undertaken within the bounds of caution.* Entry points agreed as (a) Grue's Pit, (b) Tunnels from Camden Lock line to Beasley's Great Hall, (c) From King's Cross to the Bridge over Beasley's Basin. [This was the bridge noted by Jen, and the line it carried had been disused since the Beasley Loop was constructed to give access to the Camden line without cutting across the Canallers' territory. However, after discussion it was thought to be still usable for most of its length, and this indeed proved to be the case.]

3. *It is agreed to announce a Parliament at Camden Lock.* This Parliament to decide how the Battle should be

concluded, and to deal with all the differences that led to it; BUT, that this Parliament should not be held until Items 1 and 2 have been dealt with as thoroughly as possible.

* * *

For the sake of clarity in this précis, it is proposed to deal first with Item 2, since we already have foreknowledge of the inevitable outcome of Item 1.

The first party to actually see the Rats was that from Camden Lock to the Great Hall tunnels, and they reported back with three interesting observations. The first was that the Rats were only very cautiously exploring the tunnels leading off the Great Hall and the impression gained was that they didn't really want to penetrate further. Second, the Rats seemed to be staying together in fairly large groups, and third, that although the Rats did not attack the Search Party, every member of that party was agreed that they would have received short shrift if they themselves had attempted to attack the Rats.

The second party to arrive came from Kings Cross and they were able to observe the Rats' behaviour with more leisure since they were forty feet above them on the Basin Bridge. Their conclusions were that, although the Rats were in total control of the Basin, they seemed more interested in making a home there than going beyond it up the Primrose Canal. Nor were they making efforts to climb the Basin Bridge, even when they saw the train above them.

The last party to arrive were naturally the Grue's Pit party, since they had to go right back to Savernake Road and take Dingle's Old Route. [As a matter of interest, it was noted that Dingle himself acted as Guide again, having presumably enjoyed his previous period of command sufficiently to wish to repeat it.] They reported Grue's Pit itself as clear but the Arches as completely taken over. They had been able to get right up to the broken ramparts with no attack being made, although everyone remarked, quite independently, that they felt that one step further forward into the Arches would have been fiercely resisted. They remained there for some while before returning, and even tried to get the *Flying Blogger* repaired sufficiently to be able to back it out, but alas to no avail.

The Captain and Bloggs discussed these findings and agreed that, for the moment at least, the Rats seemed more interested in establishing themselves in the more roomy and commodious home of the Arches than in trying to spread themselves throughout the system. That this made it necessary to abandon Beasley's Arches was a severe blow to the Captain above all, but, short of an all-out war, the outcome of which would have been doubtful, there seemed no alternative.

The question of the Abovegrounders was far more vexed because far more unpredictable. The search itself was thorough to a degree. Never, in the history of the system, had so many engines, narrow-boats and barges been out at one time. The congestion was appalling, and three accidents were reported in the first half-hour. All passing places were jammed full and narrow-boats had often to wedge themselves into communication tunnels to let other boats through.

The communication tunnels themselves were a special interest of the Captain, who rightly saw them as natural hiding-holes for the Abovegrounders, given that they managed to find a boat, and he sent Couriers by the dozen to explore every one.

Bloggs' mind worked differently, and when the twelve hours of searching had produced nothing, he suspected that they had got out of the North London system altogether and were already far on their way down the Western Line, via Primrose Hill or possibly via the Primrose Canal and East Heath.

He and the Captain maintained their Headquarters at

Camden Lock, although, to avoid overcrowding, the bulk of the Long Shafters returned home and the Beasley's Canallers were split between Camden and Shipley's Basin. There was no doubt in anyone's mind, however, that the Beasley's men would have to be properly resettled, and the Captain was already negotiating for a new base at the Northern end of the New Junction and Primrose Canals.

When Bloggs' enquiries far down the Western line produced a blank, and three days of searching the North London system was equally non-productive, he and the Captain were forced to consider the possibility that Widgie and Jen had escaped Above.

This was a question of the utmost seriousness, bringing with it the strong probability of invasion by the Above-grounders in force, for the idea that Widgie and Jen would not relate their experiences was so remote as to be un-believable.

In the light of this, various defensive measures were adopted—Ventilation Shafts, already cunningly concealed were, in many cases, blocked up completely; Observation Shafts (the Bumps) of which there were only eight in the entire system, were maintained because they were considered essential, but a new system of double-locking was incorporated in their design. A standing guard was mounted twenty-four hours a day at each Shaft, and elaborate plans for the evacuation of the whole system were made, should it prove necessary.

Eventually it was considered unwise to delay the promised Parliament any longer, and Bloggs and the Captain issued a joint announcement that it would take place in three days time in the Great Hall at Shipley's Basin, and that as many men as could be spared from other duties should attend.

The outcome of this Parliament was of such significance that it has been thought advisable to reproduce here certain parts of the long proceedings, which lasted in all over two-and-a-half days.

Appendix A: The End of the Story

[After the opening ceremonies, it was Bloggs who was allowed to put the most important question before the meeting.]

Bloggs: If this 'ere Parliament may now be considered open, I will put forward the question vital to all: Given that the Battle for Beasley's Arches were interrupted by an Armistice called for by the Captain 'ere, how should we resolve the matter? As we of the Railway sees it, we 'ave been robbed of a victory which should 'ave resulted in the Arches being 'anded over to us, and ...

Captain: And as we of the Canal sees it, the Arches was built by Canallers and for Canallers and 'as been subjected to continual harassment by the Railway since 1892 if me memory serves me right—I could refer to the Records—of which the latest attack was but another outrageous example. Thus we see the attackers as the guilty party and thus 'aving no rights anyways, Armistice or no.

Bloggs: 'Aving no *rights*? You says 'aving no *rights*? May I remind you, Mister Captain, that we used to 'ave a station at Beasley's? I says *used* to 'ave, Mister Captain, and I have little doubt you'll remember who forced us out of it.

Captain: That station should never 'ave been built, Bloggs, and you know it. 'Twas an act of provocation. You 'ad no need of that station, Bloggs, and what's more you proved it later when you built the Beasley Link to by-pass it.

Voice: Why shouldn't we have 'ad a station at Beasley's? Ain't nothing in the Rules that says not.

Voice: Canallers built Beasley's that's why not.

Voice: Ay, and Railway built Long Shaft but it didn't stop you lot building Highgate Canal at top end.

Voice: Get back to the point—who let Rats out of

213

Grue's Pit?

Voice: Ay—and who put 'em in there in first place?

Voice: But who let 'em breed before that? Canallers. Allus bred in Canals, they did.

Voice: Ay, and ye left the Railway to clear 'em up.

Voice: Clear 'em up? Sent 'em to Grue's Pit to get us out of Beasley's more likely.

Voice: Stick to the point—who lost the Abovegrounders, I'd like to know?

[. . . Meeting broke up in disorder. Parliament re-convened three hours later.]

Smoker: I 'as asked permission to speak from both Bloggs and the Cap'n and this 'ere permission were granted, and I'm sure I'm very grateful being only a younger, though me Dad was Chief Driver at Great North Road. And what I says is, we're trying to decide rights and wrongs what can't be decided 'cos they goes back so far. And even when they don't, who can decide rights and wrongs between Bloggs and the Cap'n, what with Horns being blown and Captain's Hundreds and Abovegrounders. So I says this be all too complicated for my little brain, (as me Dad allus said I never did 'ave much), and I votes that too much History and going back and all, and too much talk about who was right in the Big Battle —and it *was* a Big Battle—does us no good, and what we needs is to stop fighting and arguing among ourselves, and let's rebuild Beasley's somewhere else instead and build up defences against them Abovegrounders. And let's treat them Rats decent-like—'cos we've all got to live down 'ere together with never a glimpse of the sun save at Long Shaft—and what I say is that this 'ere Big Battle oughter be *used*. Ay, that's it, I knew there was a point somewhere if I

could only find it. Let's *use* the Big Battle to
get together and get on with it, 'stead of
worrying about who won it, 'cos Rats won it
anyway, and I thanks you Bloggs and you
Cap'n for permission to speak.

* * *

There followed another day-and-a-half's discussion, but at
the end of it Smoker's motion, such as it was, was written
up in proper language and signed by both parties, and it
appeared to open up a new period of co-operation and
construction between the Canal and the Railway.

The threat of invasion from Above gradually receded as
weeks passed with no sign of it being carried out, and,
although remembered, it became more and more forgotten.
Speculation about Widgie and Jen and their possible fate
became a subject for the Legends. Some said they drowned
in one of the Communication Tunnels, others that they
went out on the Western Line and met a fate unknown,
others that they ended up back at Beasley's and were
destroyed by the Rats.

Certainly no-one really believed that they could have
gone back Aboveground without giving the system away,
except sometimes Bloggs, who once said in public—and
oddly enough this also appears in the Records—"He were a
funny boy that Widgie. Would've made a good Railwayman,
though I says it meself. I sees 'im fight and 'e fights well.
I sees 'im jump through them flames and bring that Jumper
down with 'im, and I sees 'im with me all during the ride
through that Grue's Pit. *Talking* to 'em he was. There's
all these thousands o' Rats coming at us from all sides and
me trying to drive the old *Flying Blogger*, and 'e's *talking*
to 'em. They still attacks 'im mind, but 'e still goes on
talking. Odd.

"Don't misunderstand me—I know 'e's an Abovegrounder
and all that, but I 'ad an affection for 'im at the end. Sorry

to see 'im go, like. When my time comes and you puts me down in the Black Tunnel, I could've handed over me responsibilities to 'im. Funny that.

"So what I means is, maybe they ain't drownded or eaten or whatever. Maybe 'e got back. Wouldn't put it past 'im, and if 'e did get back neither would I put it past 'im not to talk. Never saw 'is sister, except from afar at the beginning, but 'e was fond of 'er, so I doubts not she wasn't unlike.

"Well, he's gorn and we'll never know where, so that's that; but 'e was a hindependent cuss. Ho yes, no doubt about that. Hindependent wiv a capital H."

APPENDIX B:

A Short History
of the North London System

The existence of the Little People, or Undergrounders as they are often called, has been known and documented for hundreds of years. That they are still regarded largely as a legend is a tribute to their passion for secrecy and their cunning in preserving it. Indeed, one can argue that without this secrecy they could not have survived.

In the short space of this appendix, the larger questions concerning the rise and fall of their many civilizations cannot be dealt with, it being our task to examine only a tiny section of one that arose during the early nineteenth century, namely the North London system.

The impact of the Industrial Revolution was as profound below ground as it was above. Many fascinating theories have been advanced as to why it was necessary for the Undergrounders to reflect it so exactly, but, at the end of the day, they have all led back to a simple statement: 'It was always so—imitation of the Above has always been a key factor in every one of their civilizations of which we have any knowledge.'

Over-and above this, however, there is much to be learnt from the careful way in which they examined each innovation from Above *before* they imitated it. We are forced to conclude that the Undergrounders, for all their ingenuity, were basically conservative and responded to change only with the greatest reluctance, and usually not until some sixty years later.

The North London system may be taken as an example.

Whereas they showed great cleverness in those matters peculiar to themselves, such as the growing of root vegetables or the construction and concealment of their ventilation shafts, they have so far resolutely turned down every Aboveground innovation since 1900, except one.

It should be stressed that this does not show lack of curiosity on their part—indeed, their complicated Observation Shafts stand witness to the greatest interest—nor that they are against new inventions in general. Indeed, once they have decided to copy some aspect of the Abovegrounders' life, they will spare no effort to achieve it; *vide* their cleverness in mining coal at deep levels and their success in charting underground oil fields once they decided to adopt the steam engine and the oil lamp, respectively.

We cannot look in detail at the many far-sighted ways in which the Undergrounders coped with their lot. Suffice it to say that a race, forced underground many thousands of years ago, becomes remarkably good at adjusting itself and its conditions into a form that can support tolerable life.

With the benefit of hindsight, we can say that the earliest beginnings of what we now know as the North London system go back to approximately 1800, when the North London Undergrounders, driven to rural areas by the increasing population below London, returned on visits to their parents with stories of the new canal systems being constructed Above. As they pointed out, there was no lack of water beneath London—indeed, the striking of an underground river or spring was one of the dangers to be reckoned with when extending a tunnel series—and why should it not be made use of to provide a permanent transport system?

The North Londoners listened and discussed, but could not be persuaded to move until they had actually seen a canal in operation themselves. The opportunity was soon to come, with the construction of the Grand Union Canal as far as Cumberland Basin, near King's Cross, and several new Observation Shafts were built so that these techniques of canal-building could be studied.

As the only substitute for barge-ponies available to them was man-power the scheme never came to anything, but with the introduction from Above of the steam-powered narrow-boat they renewed their interest, and the 1820s saw the introduction of several quite long stretches of canal, at the beginning providing transport between the coal and iron-ore mines and the smelting works. As the new canals also called for sluices and locks where changes of level were needed, as well as many alterations to the boats themselves to fit them for underground work—so the Undergrounders grew more curious about the many changes taking place Aboveground at that time.

The Canal Folk, as they became named, had not carried out their work without opposition, both from those who damned the canals as modern innovations and from those who believed them to be too slow and cumbersome to be worthwhile. It was the latter who were to become the visionaries, for it was they who, observing the early beginnings of London's railway systems, believed that here lay the right answer to transport below ground.

Every year, Aboveground, seemed to show an increase in railway systems and traffic; every year tracks were extended, new sidings built and new rolling-stock introduced; and finally a group of North Londoners—and actually they were very few—forced through a Parliament at Gospel Oak at which those for the Railways could discuss their plans openly with the Canal Folk.

It was a long Parliament, lasting in all ten days, and it was conducted with the thoroughness and respect for the other's point of view which was typical of the Undergrounders. In the end it was granted that the case for the Railways could not be ignored, and the Railwaymen were given permission to go ahead and put into practice all that they had learnt.

There followed six months of Committee Procedure, during which time maps were drawn up allocating tunnels to either the Railways or the Canals. Intersections caused the most bother—should the railway go over the canal at this point, or the canal over the railway by means of an aqueduct—but by the December of 1833 it was all settled and work began.

It was a period of feverish activity for the Railwaymen, and during the next twenty years they developed such an extensive layout—pushing through Bill after Bill in a series of hastily summoned Parliaments—that the Canallers began to feel that their beloved North London system was being taken over by those who had, willy-nilly, become their rivals. In the end, they decided it was time to express their views formally, and they called the now famous Parliament of 1860, at which they protested that the North London system, in the first place developed as a Canal system in the 1820s, was being tunnelled so rapidly and to such an extent by the Railwaymen that soon there would be no more space available for their own development.

This was a serious point, and one which the Railwaymen recognized; but the fact had to be faced that whereas the water available to the Canals was limited, the coal and iron-ore mines on which the Railways depended showed no signs of growing less. Furthermore, the Railwaymen pointed out, the Canal Folk could certainly have increased their network, had they had the desire to do so, by narrowing their big main canals and diverting the water in other directions. In fact, the point was made, they had shown a lack of drive.

It was true. The Canallers, at one time in the vanguard, had been left behind.

The 1860 Parliament thus had one important outcome. The Canallers realized that they had been overtaken, not by political cunning but by sheer hard work and by what for want of a better word might be called ambition. As a result they called a series of meetings at which, apart from planning several new links, they decided to make up for the limitations in their water supply by building for themselves a headquarters that would be so magnificent as to be the envy of the entire system.

Beasley's Arches was the result.

They chose the site with great care as being near enough to King's Cross to make sure of its tactical importance, whilst not getting in the way of the Railwaymen's main King's Cross line: and having chosen it they spared no expense, time or labour to build it well and grandly. It took them thirteen years to complete and during this time, and for a while afterwards, honour and everyone's sense of fairness was satisfied.

It was towards the end of the 1880s that the Railway decided that it needed a new line from Camden Lock to King's Cross, and this was generally recognized as being a useful extension, doing away as it did with the necessity for their Camden Lock traffic to go either via Paddington or northwards via Caledonian Road—this would only have been possible anyway by extending it onwards past Grue's Pit, a course of action that would have been strongly resisted by the Canallers at Beasley's. However, having taken the right and proper decision as to the best route for the new line, the Railwaymen decided to include not only a new station (at a higher level) at Beasley's, but also a bridge over the Basin at the approaches to the Arches. It was a silly and unnecessary decision, born not, perhaps, out of aggression, but certainly out of envy.

For the first time the Canallers acted decisively and to the point.

It was forbidden by the Rules to interrupt work in progress, but they called a meeting (not, it should be noted, a Parliament), in good time, at which they announced that if the Railway thrust themselves on their headquarters in this way—and they stressed that there was no actual need for the Railway to build over Beasley's, as was later born out by the Beasley Loop—they, the Canallers, would have no option but to declare outright war, and would, they gave due notice, sabotage the tracks at every opportunity.

The Railway listened and continued building.

It was now 1892 and the Canallers were as good as their word. In the next ten years they wrecked a total of twenty miles of track and Beasley's Arches changed hands thirty-eight times, as a result becoming a focal point of pride and power out of all proportion to its undoubted amenities. The war had one, and only one, thing to be said in its favour —it used up a lot of excess energy that might otherwise have been expended in enlarging the North London system into a total mess. As it was, the war, by a constant process of destruction and rebuilding, of seizing here a territory whilst giving up there a territory, became the prime mover in keeping the growth of the system within bounds.

It would be an exaggeration to say that the war lasted for another eighty years, but, as during the Hundred Years War between Britain and France, it was a period during which continual acts of small aggression flared up into considerable outbursts from time to time.

The driving of the Rats into Grue's Pit in the hope that they might invade Beasley's was a case in point; the Siege of Long Shaft another. This latter assault by the Canallers, started about three years before Widgie and Jen came on the scene, has about it several points of interest to the historian —the first going back almost to the turn of the century. Then easier communications brought about by faster transport led, over the years, to the acceptance of only two leaders for the entire North London system—one for the Railway and one for the Canals—latterly Bloggs and the Captain.

In other words, what had been a series of small communities ruling themselves and brought together by occasional Parliaments, became two overlapping states. Because the leader of one of them—Bloggs—lived in an outpost of the system, the Canallers realized that a Siege at Long Shaft that imprisoned the Railwaymen's leader, would leave the rest of the Railway at their mercy.

That this did not happen, and indeed one of the reasons why the entire Railway did not act as one to raise the Siege, was because Bloggs' lieutenants at King's Cross, Camden Lock, Paddington, etc. rather liked their new-found freedom. This was bad for the Long Shafters, but not in the end bad for the Railway, who thus showed that even if you cut off its head it was still able to stay alive. Bloggs showed his contempt for his lieutenants' behaviour by his determination to conquer Beasley's alone, and his use of Widgie and Jen's arrival as the spur to this conquest was yet another example of his forceful and political mind.

It is hard to believe that the last time an Abovegrounder penetrated the system was in 1733, when a carpenter's apprentice named Thomas Wyatt fell down a Ventilation Shaft and broke his leg, but so the Legends say. Thus the importance of Widgie and Jen's arrival, Bloggs immediate realization of it and the Captain's equally violent reaction to it led finally to the Parliament at Shipley's Basin.

Whether the peace and co-operation that followed Smoker's sensible speech will last, is still an open question, but there is little doubt that no-one would have listened to him if it hadn't been for the Rats. History is full of examples of enemies brought together by common fear or hatred of a third party, but over and above this, the Rats, by removing Beasley's Arches as a symbol of power, certainly created what might be called the geographical possibility of peace.

At the moment of writing it seems as if there might be yet another reason for optimism. It will be remembered from the Records [Bloggs/Blagfast] that the Railwaymen were using the Dead End Observation Shaft to observe the source of power developed by what they called the Little Railway—in fact the Post Office Railway.

They had first observed Electric Trains as early as 1910,

when their alarm at finding the Abovegrounders building below ground between Bishop's Road and Farringdon Street had been lessened by their pride at seeing the Abovegrounders imitating *them* for a change, but it was not until many years later that they noticed the Post Office Railway, which had, in fact, been operating since 1927. During this time, their slow but thorough minds had been working out the bases of this new power and tracing it to its source, which seemed to them to be water. They had gathered this during painstaking expeditions into rural areas as far back as 1930, and, by the time Widgie and Jen came on the scene, they felt they knew enough about it to experiment with it.

The conclusions are obvious. As long as the Ninety Year War lasted, the Railwaymen were both too proud and too sensible to approach the Canallers for something that they knew would be refused anyway. Now—and we are looking forward to something that has not yet happened—the drawing together made possible, not only by Widgie and Jen but also by the Rats, leads one to hope that the Railway may call a Parliament on the matter and propose that the Canallers allow them to harness certain of their waterways in order to provide electrical power, not only for their trains, but for general lighting for the whole system.

One is certainly looking forward, but co-operation between the Canal and the Railway would certainly help to preserve the peace won with such difficulty at the Shipley's Basin Parliament. Against this one must lay the enmity and distrust they have felt for each other for nearly a hundred years, and these enmities take a long time to die in an enclosed society. True, Bloggs and the Captain could probably resolve them, since, in the last resort, the Undergrounders are loyal to their leaders because they want to be led; but are those two forceful and ambitious characters capable of working together for a common good?

Do they, perhaps, always need a common enemy, whether it be Widgie and Jen, the Rats, or something else?